SURROUND

Your journey to put at rest the troubled spirit of the great King Silverhair has brought you to a raft in the middle of a mysterious river, said to be inhabited by fearsome monsters!

In the middle of the night, you awake with a start. Lining the shore on both sides of the raft, mere arm lengths away, gigantic, shadowy creatures stare at you with unblinking eyes, their long whiplike tongues snicking in and out in anticipation. You realize with a shudder that the creatures are giant frogs, and they could instantly snap you up like a helpless insect!

What will you do?

1) If you decide to try to frighten the frogs away, turn to page 135.

2) If you want to lie still and try to drift by the frogs, turn to page 50.

Whichever choice you make, you are sure to find adventure as you journey on your
KING'S QUEST

KING'S QUEST

BY TOM MCGOWEN

A DUNGEONS & DRAGONS™ ADVENTURE BOOK

Cover Art by Ben Otero
Interior Art by Kevin Nichols

TSR, Inc.

For Carey

KING'S QUEST
© Copyright 1984, TSR, Inc.
All Rights Reserved.

Distributed to the book trade in the United States by Random House, Inc., and in Canada by Random House of Canada, Ltd.

Distributed in the United Kingdom by TSR (UK) Ltd. Distributed to the toy and hobby trade by regional distributors.

DUNGEONS & DRAGONS and PICK A PATH TO ADVENTURE are trademarks owned by TSR, Inc.

D&D and ENDLESS QUEST are registered trademarks owned by TSR, Inc.

First printing: July, 1984
Printed in the United States of America
Library of Congress Catalog Card Number: 83-91426
ISBN: 0-88038-079-9

9 8 7 6 5 4 3 2 1

TSR, Inc.
P.O. Box 756
Lake Geneva, WI 53147

TSR (UK), Ltd.
The Mill, Rathmore Road
Cambridge CB1 4AD
United Kingdom

ou are about to set off on an adventure in which YOU will meet many dangers — and face many decisions. YOUR choices will determine how the story turns out. So be careful . . . you must choose wisely!

Do not read this book from beginning to end! Instead, as you are faced with a decision, follow the instructions and keep turning to the pages where your choices lead you until you come to an end. At any point, YOUR choice could bring success — or disaster!

You can read KING'S QUEST many times, with many different results, so if you make an unwise choice, go back to the beginning and start again!

Good luck on YOUR adventure!

In this story, you are Sparrow, a young juggler who, together with your brother, Jay, travels from town to town performing your act at inns and fairs in order to scratch out a meager existence. It's a hard life, and nothing exciting ever seems to happen to you — until today, that is. . . .

At your feet lies a dead man! In your hand is a square of parchment, upon which is drawn a crude map. You can't believe you have just agreed to undertake a quest that, if successful, will set free the tormented spirit of a king—and reward you with enormous treasure!

Only minutes ago, you and your brother, Jay, were making your way along a narrow road that winds through the vast, dim forest known as the Elfwood. Jay is seventeen, five years older than you. You are orphans, and you make a living by juggling at fairs, inns, castles—wherever you can. It's a hard life.

"We should be out of these woods by sunset, Sparrow," Jay remarked. "There's an inn near the forest's edge. Maybe they'll let us do our juggling act in exchange for supper."

Suddenly you spotted something. "There's a man lying up ahead!" you exclaimed.

You and Jay ran to where the stranger lay at the side of the road, beneath a rowan tree. Nearby, a horse nibbled grass at the edge of the woods. The middle-aged man wore the leather jacket of a warrior. You gasped as you saw an arrow protruding from his side.

"Water," he moaned weakly. "Water, I pray!"

Quickly you pulled out your water flask. He drank thirstily, then sank back weakly.

"I am dying," he whispered. "Scarface and his evil band are pursuing me. But they must not get what they seek! My only hope is to entrust it to you. Listen, and I will tell a tale that will make your hair stand on end!

"Long ago, when the great King Farad Silverhair died, he was buried in a secret tomb with his treasure, as is the custom. One day, robbers entered the tomb. They carried away the treasure and the king's bones in a bag, for there is great magic in kingly bones. They hid the bones and treasure in a cave, planning to return for it, but they never did. They were killed by a band of marauding goblins. The bones and the treasure are still there."

The stranger paused to regain his breath. "Farad Silverhair was my ancestor. His spirit cannot rest until his bones are buried again. I learned the whereabouts of the cave and was going there to bury his bones, but now I cannot. If you will swear to put him to rest, I will reveal the way. The treasure will make you rich, but you must swear to bury King Silverhair's bones. Do you swear?"

Jay studied your face intently, then nodded slowly. "We—we swear," you breathed.

The stranger fumbled in his pouch, withdrew a parchment, and placed it in your hand. "This map will show the way. But beware of Scarface and his cutthroats. They'll do anything to get the map. And when you reach the cave, beware...of the..." His words ended in a choking gasp, and he laid still.

"He's dead!" said Jay in a shocked voice.

So now you stand with the map in your hand, staring down at the dead man.

"Where does the map say the cave is, Sparrow?" asks Jay.

You study the map. "This must be the road we're on now," Jay says, pointing. The road leads to a distant town called Riverbend. Beyond the town is a cluster of hills. An arrow points to one of them. "That must be where the treasure is. Just think, Sparrow—we'll never be hungry again."

"First we must bury the king's bones," you remind him firmly. "And remember, he tried to warn us about some kind of danger at the cave. I wonder what that could be. . . ."

You have no tools to bury the dead man, but you're sure the elves who live in the forest will find him and bury him. You gently close his eyes and fold his hands over his chest.

"Come on," says Jay. "If this road leads to that town, all we have to do is stay on it!"

"Not necessarily," you say hesitantly. "The stranger said someone was after him. That must be who shot him with the arrow! If we stay on the road, we may run into them. We'd be safer traveling among the trees."

"I don't think so, Sparrow. This forest belongs to the elves, and they don't like having humans in it. People can go through as long as they stay on the road, but if we leave it, we could get into trouble with the elves!"

1) If you decide to stay on the road, turn to page 32.

2) If you decide to travel through the forest, turn to page 35.

You awaken to find Rogaldo preparing a hearty breakfast for you. After eating, you start out, expecting to follow the river until you come to a bridge. But to your surprise, Rogaldo walks straight down the riverbank to the river's edge. "Follow me," he calls.

"How will we go over the river?" Jay asks.

"We won't. We'll go UNDER it!" the wizard says with a smile. "I've cast a spell to surround us with a shell of air."

"But what about the creatures?" you ask.

"They're all far upstream," he assures you.

Crossing the river is like walking through a glass tunnel. When you emerge onto the other bank, your clothes aren't even damp.

An hour later, you come to a road and follow it until it splits off in two directions.

"We must make a choice here," Rogaldo explains. "Both roads meet the main road into Riverbend. The right-hand road takes three days through a great plain where some dangerous creatures dwell. The other road takes over a day through a desert, where many very dangerous things live. So the road through the plain has less danger but for a longer time. The desert offers more danger but for a shorter time. Which shall it be?"

1) If you decide to take the long way through the plain, turn to page 106.

2) If you decide to take the short way through the desert, turn to page 118.

You decide it's safest to sleep in a tree. You find one with thick branches and climb it.

But you don't sleep well. It grows so dark that you can't see your hand two feet away, and the forest is full of frightening sounds.

When morning comes, you climb down sleepily and ask, "Which way is the road, Jay?"

"This way, I think," he says, pointing. But after traveling for some time, you both realize that you should have reached the road by now.

"I'm afraid we're lost," you say miserably.

"We've got to find the way out!" he says determinedly. "We could starve to death if we don't. We just have to keep looking, Sparrow!"

"Well, well. Lost and starving, eh? That's too bad," says a small, high voice. You look about quickly. Seated upon a nearby tree branch is a little man, no more than two feet tall, with gauzy green wings. It's a pixie!

"Just follow me, and I promise that your worries will soon be over," it says sincerely.

You and Jay both know that pixies are most untrustworthy. But maybe this one really does want to help you. Should you trust the pixie, or should you keep looking for the way out of the forest yourselves?

1) If you decide to trust the pixie, turn to page 42.

2) If you decide you can't trust the pixie, turn to page 85.

Hesitating only a moment, you dash out the door. You run until your side aches and you gasp for breath. Slowing to a walk, you hope that somehow the red-bearded man manages to defeat his three opponents.

The sound of hooves thunders through the night air somewhere behind you. You turn to see three black-clad figures galloping toward you! Redbeard must not have survived!

Desperately you search for somewhere to hide, but there is only open meadow. You know you can't outrun the horses, so you simply wait for the riders to reach you, trying hard not to show how frightened you are.

The riders rein in their horses, and the scarfaced man holds out his hand. "I think you have a certain map," he says coldly. "Give it to me and you can live. Tell me another lie and I'll kill you and find it anyway!"

Wordlessly you take the map from your pouch and hand it to Scarface. He unfolds it, gives it a quick glance, then tucks it into his belt. With a grunted command, the riders spur their horses and gallop on up the road.

You know now that the spirit of King Silverhair may never find rest, and your dreams of riches are gone forever. But at least you're still alive. With a sigh, you trudge back toward the inn. Perhaps Redbeard is still alive and you can make up for running away. And perhaps Jay will turn up in a day or so. . . .

THE END

You make your way along the riverbank, peering about for any sign of dangerous creatures. Soon you realize you're in a huge marsh, with a forest of cattails and bulrushes stretching out on both sides of the river. The marsh resounds with strange sounds.

Once you think you see the huge scaly shape of a dinosaur in the distance. Another time, a big shaggy, shambling thing, like a pile of rotting plants with two legs, stares at you from the other side of the river. But when morning arrives, the night noises die away, as if all the dreadful creatures of the swamp have gone into hiding for the day. By midmorning, you have left the marsh behind.

You trudge on all day without seeing a sign of life. But when twilight begins to turn into night once more, you see lights twinkling ahead and know you are nearing Riverbend. You reach the town sometime later and find a stable to sleep in, with soft hay for a bed.

The next morning, with the last of your money, you buy a spear for each of you and start out on the last leg of your quest into the desolate hilly country beyond town.

By late afternoon, you have found the hill, and you begin the long climb to the top. Suddenly Jay stops and asks, "Did you hear that?"

You listen for a moment before you hear a deep rumbling noise that rises and falls. It seems to be coming from the crest of the hill.

"We'd better not make any noise until we

find out what that is," says Jay in a low voice.

Carefully you continue up the hillside, the noise growing louder all the while. Finally, as you make your way around a large boulder, you see what is making the sound.

On the rocky slope, no more than a hundred steps away, is a cave. And lying in the entrance, its gigantic body half inside and half outside, is a huge slumbering dragon! The sound you have been hearing is its breathing!

You stare in dismay. The creature's jaws are as long as your whole body, and it is covered with gleaming brownish scales that look as hard as a metal shield. From its nostrils, thin trickles of pale blue smoke cloud the air.

You feel Jay pull at your arm, and he jerks his head toward the slope behind you. He wants to move back down the trail to talk. You nod, and as quietly as possible, the two of you steal back down the hillside out of earshot.

"Sparrow," Jay whispers, "we don't have a chance against that dragon! There's only one thing we can do—give up!"

You shake your head firmly. "There are two other things we could do, Jay. One is to wait to see if the dragon leaves. And the other is to try to talk to it!"

1) If you decide to wait to see if the dragon leaves, turn to page 21.

2) If you decide to talk to the dragon, turn to page 16.

Slowly you reach into your pouch, pull out the map, and drop it into Redbeard's hand. "Jay has taken care of me since I was little," you explain, "and he's usually right. I've got to do what he thinks is best."

Redbeard nods and smiles gently. "I understand, Sparrow, and I think you're lucky to have a brother who takes such good care of you. I promise to bury King Farad's bones as you would have. And I'll tell you what . . ."

He pulls off his belt pouch, full of his share of the gold coins you found in the wight's den, and sets it before you with a thump. "If I should get killed going after the treasure, I certainly won't be needing this! And if I come back with the king's treasure, I won't need it either. So if I'm lucky, we'll all be rich enough—and King Farad will sleep in peace, too."

"I—I hope you find the treasure and come back safely, Redbeard," you tell him. And somehow, you're sure that he will!

THE END

"TALK to it?" exclaims Jay, startled. Glancing fearfully up toward the top of the hill, he drops his voice to a whisper again. "You're crazy, Sparrow! What makes you think you could talk to that—that thing?"

"Dragons can talk just like we do, Jay. And not all of them are evil. I think that's a gold dragon—one of the good ones."

"What would you say?" asks Jay.

"I'd ask it to let us have the bones of Farad Silverhair so we could bury them," you tell him. "We promised to do that, Jay, and we've got to try! If that dragon believes in lawful good, it will give us the bones."

"And if it's evil, it'll burn us to a crisp!" Jay says grimly. He thinks for a few moments, then draws a deep breath. "Well, I can't let you go by yourself, Sparrow. If we're going to die, we may as well die together. Come on."

Leaving your spears behind, you walk back up to the crest of the hill. You don't know about Jay, but your legs are shaking so that you can hardly walk! You and Jay come to a halt about twenty steps from the dragon. Fearfully you clear your throat, hoping the sound will awaken the creature.

One of the dragon's eyes snaps open suddenly. It is deep yellow and as big as your head! A moment later, the other eyes opens. "Now, what in the name of dragondom is THIS?" demands the puzzled dragon in a deep, rumbling voice.

So far, so good, you think. You're sure that if

this dragon were evil, you and Jay would be dead by now. In a trembling voice you say, "Sir Dragon, may we please talk to you?"

The dragon stares at you for a few moments more. Then it says, "What do you want to talk to me about, little one?"

You tell the dragon everything, from your meeting with the dying man in the forest right up to the present moment. "We—we were hoping you'd let us have the bones of King Farad Silverhair so we could end his spirit's sorrow and keep our promise," you finish in a rush.

"So THAT'S what's causing all that moaning at night in the cave!" the dragon roars. "Young human, I am touched by your sad tale—and also by your bravery. I will let you take the bones of the king, and you may also take one of the treasure chests from the cave."

You and Jay stare at each other in amazement. This is more than you could have hoped for!

"Hold out your torch," orders the dragon. Jay removes the torch from his belt and holds it out toward the dragon. With a gentle snort, the dragon sets the end of it ablaze, then stands aside from the entrance to the cave.

"You'll find it quite safe in there," it says. "There was a large spider living in the cave when I first came, but a few fiery puffs took care of that problem."

You hurry into the cave, down a short, rocky passage and into a large cavern. By the light from the torch, you see a pile of chests and bags in one corner. You feel the bags until you find one that is filled with bones and pick it up. Jay grabs a small chest filled with glittering gold coins and sparkling jewels. Then you hurry back out of the cave.

You want the dragon to know that you appreciate its kindness and bow deeply. "Thank you very, very much, Sir Dragon. You are one of the kindest persons—er, dragons—I ever met."

"You're welcome, little one," says the dragon. "Now be off with you, and don't tell any other humans about this! I don't want mobs of them coming up here and bothering me."

It's nearly dusk when you and Jay reach the bottom of the hill. Using your spears, you quickly dig a grave for the bones of King Farad Silverhair.

"You did it, Sparrow!" exclaims Jay. "If it hadn't been for you, I'd have just given up. I'd never have dreamed of trying to talk to a dragon!"

"We were lucky, Jay," you say happily. "We've kept our promise to bury the king, and we have enough treasure to make things easy for us for the rest of our lives. I'd say it was a pretty successful quest!"

THE END

"I think we should get out of here as fast as we can, Redbeard," you tell him. "Every extra moment we spend here, we're in danger!"

Redbeard sighs. "You're probably right. Let's get going, then."

You hurry through the darkness for what seems like forever. Finally the hills are behind you and the sky is turning faintly pink. "We're safe now," says Redbeard. His mouth stretches into an enormous yawn. "Are you as tired as I am? We can sleep awhile if you'd like." Gratefully you sink down into the soft grass.

You awaken at midday and share a quick meal of bread and cheese with Redbeard.

"Listen, Sparrow," says the warrior as he eats, "there are two ways we can get to Riverbend from here. We can go back to the road and follow it into town, but Scarface and his gang may be watching the road.

"The other way is to keep going straight to the river. There's a ford we can cross and then go on to Riverbend. The only trouble with that plan is that there are tales of a nixie who guards the ford and enslaves people who try to cross." He eyes you for a moment. "Which would you rather risk—the road or the ford?"

1) If you choose to cross at the ford, turn to page 73.

2) If you choose to go back to the road, turn to page 87.

"What makes you think the dragon will go away?" whispers Jay.

"Well, it has to eat sometime," you point out. "It probably hunts deer and other animals. While it's gone, we can get into the cave, get King Farad's bones and some of the treasure, and be gone before it comes back."

Jay stares at you thoughtfully for a few moments, then nods. "All right, Sparrow. Let's give it a try. I hate to think of giving up when we've come this close."

You sneak cautiously back up toward the crest of the hill and crouch behind the boulder to spy on the dragon. You watch silently as the afternoon turns to evening and the surrounding hills become shrouded in twilight.

Finally the dragon awakens. Its yellow eyes flash open, it gives a tremendous yawn, and then it heads straight down the hillside and vanishes in the gathering darkness.

"Quick, Jay, light the torch!" you urge. Jay removes the torch from his belt and lights it with flint and steel. Then the two of you race toward the cave.

"I hope there's nothing else in the cave," you pant. "I'm not convinced this dragon is what the dying man was trying to warn us of."

"If there was anything, the dragon probably got rid of it," Jay says hopefully. "Anyway, it's no time to worry about it now!"

You pass through the cave entrance, hurry through a short passageway, and enter a large cavern. In the flickering torchlight, you see a pile of bags and chests in one corner. Quickly you run your hands over the bags until you feel the one that contains King Silverhair's bones.

"I have the king's bones," you tell Jay. "We can bury them as soon as we get far enough away. I wish he knew how much trouble we've gone to to help him!"

Jay tucks a small chest under his free arm and says, "Come on. Let's get out of here!"

You dash back through the passageway and out the entrance—only to find yourselves face-to-face with the dragon, crouched before the cave, its yellow eyes blazing in fury!

"So!" it roars in a voice that makes the hill shudder. "Thieves!"

Frozen with terror, you stare up at the huge creature, knowing it intends to kill you!

Suddenly a strange, pale vapor begins to swirl from the bag you are holding. Swiftly it forms into the figure of a tall, elderly man with long, pale hair, dressed in armor and wearing a crown. The figure glows eerily in the darkness, and you know you are looking at the spirit of King Farad Silverhair!

"Dragon," it says in a voice that is only a thin whisper, "in the name of lawful good, I call upon you to spare these youngsters!"

"Why should I spare them, spirit?" demands the dragon. "They are merely thieves."

"They are not truly thieves," whispers the spirit. "They have braved many dangers to set my spirit free so that I may at last rest in

peace. They felt there was no other way but to steal into the cave while you were gone. Their intentions were honorable, not evil. I pray you, let them bury my bones so that my torment will be brought to an end!"

The dragon hesitates a moment, then says, "Very well. They may keep your bones and their lives, but that is all! No treasure!"

"No," whispers the spirit. "They shall also have my blessing, and that may be worth a great deal to them, dragon." And before your eyes, the image fades and is gone.

Your legs are trembling, but you realize the ghost has saved your lives. Jay sets the treasure chest down, and you hurry away from the glaring dragon. At the boulder, you pick up your spears and continue on down the hill.

At the bottom of the hill, you dig a grave with your spears and carefully bury the bag containing King Farad Silverhair's bones. At long last, you have kept your pledge, and the quest is finished.

"He saved our lives, Jay," you murmur. "I'm glad we could help him."

"I'm glad we brought the king peace at last," Jay agrees. "But I wish we could have taken some of the treasure. I guess we're just meant to be poor all our lives, Sparrow."

"I don't know, Jay," you say thoughtfully. "King Farad's blessing just might turn out to be worth a lot more than we realize!"

THE END

The sun is well up in the sky and the Haunted Vale is far behind when you reach the ford that crosses the river. Exhausted, you and Redbeard snatch a quick nap, awakening around noontime. Redbeard sits on the grassy riverbank and pulls off his boots.

"The water is no more than knee-deep at this time of year," he says. "No use getting your shoes soaked, lad. Pull 'em off and carry 'em."

You remove your shoes as he tucks his boots under his arm and marches into the water. You follow and give a squeal of shock when you step into the cold water, but you quickly get used to it. Moving carefully so you won't slip and fall, you wade along at Redbeard's side.

You are in the middle of the broad river when Redbeard gives a loud gasp. He stops, staring downstream. There, out in the deeper part of the river, a figure has suddenly appeared and is moving swiftly toward you. It looks like a man, but its body is completely covered with pale green fishlike scales. Its hands are webbed like the feet of a frog, and its eyes are large and staring. A nixie!

You have heard of these creatures. They live at the bottoms of lakes and rivers in beautiful palaces, and they keep humans as slaves. Nixies have the power to enchant humans, robbing them of their will so they must obey. They enchant their captives so that they are able to live and breathe underwater. If this nixie plans to enchant you and Redbeard, you could become its slaves for the rest of your lives!

"We can't escape—it can move faster than we can!" groans Redbeard.

"Can you use your silver dagger?" you ask.

"That will only work against creatures of darkness," says Redbeard bleakly. "I fear there is no hope."

You wait for the nixie's spell to steal over you, but nothing happens. As the creature draws nearer, you can see that it seems puzzled.

"Its magic isn't working for some reason!" exclaims Redbeard. He whips out the sword he took from the wight's lair. "Well, then, it'll have to fight me to get me!"

At the sight of the sword, the nixie stops dead in its tracks. Then it gives an enraged hiss, plunges into the water, and is gone!

Redbeard stares after it, then peers at the sword. It is glowing faintly, and a loud humming sound fills the air. Gradually the glow and the hum fade away.

Redbeard gives a loud whoop. "This must be a magic sword, Sparrow. It has power against its owner's enemies! Lucky for us we went into that wight's den, or we'd be breathing water by now. Come on, let's get out of this cursed river."

You wade to shore and dry your feet in the tall grass, warm from the sunshine, and don your shoes again. Then you and Redbeard strike out toward Riverbend, which you can just see far in the distance.

You reach town late in the afternoon, and your spirits soar in anticipation of finding your brother here. Jay probably got out of the forest long before you did, and when he didn't find you at the inn, he must have taken the road toward town. He knows the hills beyond town are where the cave is. Why, he's probably been waiting for you since morning!

But as you and Redbeard walk up and down the streets, peering into inns and courtyards, you see no sign of Jay. You hurry to the bridge to look for him, but he isn't there, either.

"We must have got here ahead of him, Sparrow," says Redbeard consolingly. "He may not have gotten out of the forest as soon as you did. He may still be behind us."

"What if he didn't get out of the forest at all?" you say, your voice choking. "What if he's still there, or in danger somewhere?"

"We can wait here for him, Sparrow," says Redbeard. "Or else, first thing tomorrow, we can go find the cave, bury poor Farad's bones, take the treasure, and then look for your brother. What do you want to do?"

1) If you want to wait to see if Jay comes before going to look for the treasure, turn to page 121.

2) If you want to finish the quest first, then look for Jay, turn to page 152.

You decide that it's just too dangerous to try to help the bear. After all, you have enough trouble already, without maybe getting an arm or leg chewed up, too! You turn away and begin to trudge through the forest, peering between the trees for any sight of the road.

As time goes on, you become more and more worried. You begin to fear that you could wander about in these woods until you die of hunger and thirst. To make matters worse, the sun is setting, and the forest is deepening with shadows. It will soon be night.

Suddenly you realize that some of the shadows at the periphery of your vision are moving! You stop dead and peer about through the trees, a chill of terror gripping you. You are surrounded by dark, four-footed shapes that stare back at you with gleaming yellow eyes. A wolf pack!

The wolves form a circle around you as you stand petrified with fear. Slowly, silently, they begin to slink toward you, and you realize with a shock that this is . . .

THE END

You feel it will be safest to sleep on the ground without a fire. When night comes, the forest turns black, full of frightening noises. However, somehow you manage to fall asleep.

You're awakened by a sharp pain in your side, as if someone has kicked you. You scramble to your knees, and in the gray light of dawn, you see that you are surrounded by a band of squat, misshapen creatures with hideous faces. They wear raggedy furs and chain mail armor, and they are armed with swords, spears, axes, and shields. Goblins!

One of the goblins yells something in a strange-sounding language and yanks you to your feet. Quickly it ties your hands together in front of you, then pushes you and Jay among a cluster of slim, pale-haired people you recognize as elves. Their hands, too, are tied. "What's going on?" you ask one of them.

"It's a goblin raiding party," the elf says. "They'll take us to their caverns to be slaves."

One of the goblins orders you to be silent, and the band breaks into a trot, pushing their captives along with them. As the morning goes on, the goblins move steadily through the forest. Around noon, you cross a shallow stream, and a short while later, you are out of the forest, moving across a broad plain.

Around midafternoon, the goblins begin jabbering excitedly. You become aware of a large number of men on horseback galloping across the plain toward you, and your heart leaps. Perhaps they're coming to your rescue!

The goblins halt and begin to hop up and down, waving their weapons at the approaching horsemen. The mounted warriors smash into the goblins, slashing with their curved swords. In a few brief moments, the goblins are wiped out!

The warriors dismount and free all of you. "We're sure glad to see YOU!" you exclaim. "Who are you? Where did you come from?"

"This is our land, and we are border guards," he explains. "It's lucky for you that our scouts spotted that band of goblins, or you'd have been slaves for the rest of your lives. Who are you? How did they capture you?"

"We're jugglers," Jay tells him. "We stopped to sleep and the goblins found us."

"Jugglers, eh?" says the man. "Our king loves juggling. Why don't you come back to our city with us and do your act for him? I'm sure he'd pay you well."

You and Jay look at one another. You both know you ought to keep on with your quest, but do you dare refuse these men who have rescued you? What if they are offended?

1) If you decide to accept the warrior's invitation and accompany your rescuers to their city, turn to page 145.

2 If you decide to refuse the invitation and continue on with your quest, turn to page 59.

You don't want to risk trouble with the elves. Besides, the dead man's murderers may not be in the forest at all, so you decide to stay on the road. You fold up the map, stuff it into your belt pouch, and start out. Before you've gone a hundred steps, there's a sudden drumming of hooves, and half a dozen riders on horseback thunder around a curve straight toward you!

Jay dodges to one side of the road and you dart to the other, but at a word from their leader, they pull their horses to a halt and stare down at you.

As you examine them, you decide they are a dangerous-looking crew. There are six in all, but three aren't even human—two have the ugly features of half-orcs, and one is a snarling, hyena-faced gnoll. All wear hooded black cloaks, with long swords hanging from their belts and bows slung over their shoulders.

"Did you pass a rider on the road?" asks the leader, flicking his glance from you to Jay. He has a black beard, and a puckered white scar runs up one cheek.

"Someone passed us a ways back," you tell him, hoping they'll ride on.

He eyes you silently for a moment, then barks, "They're lying! Seize them!"

"Run for it, Sparrow," Jay yells as he darts into the woods on his side of the road. You turn and scurry into the woods on the opposite side. Behind you, you hear shouts and curses. You glance back to see that several of them have

dismounted from their horses and are crashing through the underbrush after you. You weave in and out among the trees at breakneck speed until at last the sounds of pursuit grow fainter. Finally you stop, gasping for breath. You listen for any sound of your pursuers, but you hear nothing.

As you look around, your heart sinks. You are deep in the woods, and you have no idea where the road is. You're lost!

You wander among the trees, hoping desperately that you'll stumble across the road. Suddenly you become aware of a faint whining sound, and you peer about to see what's making it. You spot a dead tree lying on the ground, and caught beneath it, amid a tangle of branches, is a young bear, little more than a cub. A gust of wind must have blown the tree down and trapped the animal. As you watch, the bear scrabbles frantically with its front paws but can't free itself.

You could easily free the cub. You hate to see a helpless, frightened animal. On the other hand, if you try to help the bear, it may only turn on you. Although it's fairly small, it could still injure you with its sharp teeth. What should you do?

1) If you decide it's too risky to help the bear cub, turn to page 28.

2) If you decide to ignore the risk and help the bear cub, turn to page 130.

It seems to you as if there's more to be feared from the murderers the dying man was fleeing than from the stern but fair elves, so you decide to leave the road and head into the forest.

You make your way through the trees until you are some distance from the road but can still see it. Suddenly you hear the sound of hooves. You crouch low and, peering through the trees, see half a dozen horsemen ride by. They are dressed in black hooded cloaks, with swords hanging from their belts and bows slung across their shoulders. Three are not even human—there are two ugly half-orcs and one snarling, hyena-faced gnoll. It looks like a dangerous crew!

"They must be the ones the stranger was fleeing from," whispers Jay.

You decide to move on, still keeping the road in sight. But after a short time, you hear hooves again. Three of the hooded riders come into sight, moving slowly, leaning down off their horses to peer at the ground and glance into the woods. You and Jay both know they are looking for you! They must have been able to tell from your footprints that someone had been with the dying man and now has the map. They're trying to track you!

Suddenly the men come to a stop and start to dismount, as if they are going to come into the forest straight toward you!

Like startled rabbits, you and Jay dash deeper into the woods, leaping over logs and ducking under low limbs. Finally you come to a stop, panting.

"I think we're safe," Jay says hopefully.

You look around. You are in a small clearing, but all you can see around you is a wall of tree trunks. "Where's the road, Jay?"

"Straight back that way, I think," says Jay, pointing. "Don't worry. We'll find it. I think we'd better stay here awhile, though, to make sure those guys don't find us."

You look around again. The forest is starting to fill with shadows. "It's going to be dark pretty soon, Jay. We can't look for the road in the dark. We're going to have to spend the night here. Is it safe?"

"We can make a fire to scare off any animals," he says, then frowns. "Of course, those bandits might see it. . . . Maybe we could climb a tree and sleep in it."

"We might fall out," you say dubiously.

"Well, we could always sleep on the ground without a fire and hope nothing dangerous comes along," says Jay. "You decide, Sparrow."

1) If you decide to sleep on the ground with a fire, turn to page 91.

2) If you decide to sleep in a tree, turn to page 10.

3) If you decide to sleep on the ground without a fire, turn to page 30.

It's not an easy choice, but you decide you'd rather take a chance on ghosts than on monsters. "Let's try to make it through the Haunted Vale," you tell Redbeard.

As soon as it is completely dark, you and Redbeard sneak away from the campfire, cross the road, and make off across the field. For a long time, you trudge through the darkness side by side. Then you begin to see the slopes of hills rising, gray in the moonlight, on each side of you. You are entering the Haunted Vale!

"Stay behind me," mutters Redbeard. He draws his sword, and his head is in constant motion as he darts nervous glances in every direction. "Make sure nothing sneaks up behind us," he tells you.

You should be sleepy at this time of night, but fear and excitement keep you wide awake. Clutching the hem of Redbeard's leather tunic, you peer anxiously about, looking for some sign of movement on the moonlit hillsides or the inky black patches of shadow that mottle the valley floor, all the while praying that you won't see anything.

Out of the darkness comes a hideous, drawn-out wail that rises to a shriek, then fades away: "ooooOOOOAAAaaa . . ."

"What's that?" you whisper.

"Let's just hope we never find out!" Redbeard whispers back.

The wail is repeated, this time nearer: "oooOOOAAaaa . . ."

You and Redbeard halt, peering through the darkness. Is that something moving toward you in the shadows? Yes! You can make out a dim shape lurching swiftly and purposefully through the tall grass. It enters a patch of moonlight, and you gasp in horror as you see it clearly. It looks something like a man, but its body is like a skeleton with skin stretched tightly over its bones. It is clothed in tattered, rotting rags. Stringy white hair hangs lankly around its gaunt face, and its eyes burn with an eerie red glow!

"What is THAT?" you squeak.

"A wight," Redbeard replies grimly. "Loathsome undead creatures that dwell in ancient graves and hate all living humans."

"Can you kill it with your sword?" you ask hopefully.

"No," he answers. "Creatures of the living dead can't be destroyed by ordinary weapons."

The thing is nearly upon you now. A horrible odor, like the smell of rotting meat, meets your nostrils, making you gag. You can see now its sharp fangs and claws! It gives another horrible wail that sends a cold shiver down the length of your back.

Quickly Redbeard reaches down into his boot and withdraws a small dagger. Its blade gleams bright in the moonlight.

"What good will a dagger do if a sword can't kill the monster," you wonder to yourself. But Redbeard holds the dagger perched in midair, and with a snap of his wrist, he hurls it

straight into the creature's chest. Suddenly
the wight simply vanishes! Nothing is left of
it but a small pile of the foul rags it wore!

"How—how did you do that?" you ask in
wonder.

"My dagger is made of silver," Redbeard
explains, bending over to pick the dagger out
of the pile of rags. "A long time ago I learned
that silver or magical weapons are the only
way that wights, werewolves, and other such
undead things can be destroyed—and I made
sure I had the means in case I ever met up
with one."

Redbeard slips the dagger back into his boot
and looks around. "Listen, Sparrow, the
longer we stay in this vale, the more likely we
are to run into some other dreadful creature,
but this wight's lair must be nearby somewhere, and I think we ought to take the time
to look for it. A wight's lair is usually in an
ancient grave, and there is often treasure in
such places. What do you say—shall we look
for the lair, or shall we just get out of here
before we bump into something else?"

1) If you decide to search for the wight's
   lair, turn to page 61.

2) If you decide against searching for the
   lair so you can get out of this awful
   place sooner, turn to page 20.

"We can't risk it—attack!" you declare.

Rogaldo lifts his arms high, and you see a bolt of lightning brighter than daylight, followed by an earsplitting burst of thunder.

Incredibly, the dragon dodges the bolt. With a shriek of fury, it swoops toward you, its terrible claws outstretched.

"Run for it!" shouts Rogaldo. "I'll hold it off as long as I can."

You race into the desert. When you glance back, all you see is a thick, yellowish cloud.

"Poor Rogaldo!" you exclaim.

"Poor US!" pants Jay. "When that dragon is finished with him, it'll come after us!"

You run until you can run no more. Gasping, you throw yourselves down behind a bush. The yellow smoke is spreading out over the entire desert, obscuring any hint of what is happening. Finally the smoke clears, but you see no sign of the wizard or the dragon.

"I guess we're back on our own now," Jay says, rising to his feet. "Come on, Sparrow. Let's head back to the road."

Side by side, you trudge back toward the road. Suddenly the ground seems to split open in front of you, and a huge pointed head appears, its enormous mouth bristling with sharp teeth. You realize with deepening terror that it is a bulette—a land shark! Maybe Rogaldo could have stopped it with his magic, but for the two of you, it looks like . . .

THE END

You decide you have no choice but to trust the pixie. Otherwise you may wander in the forest until you die.

You watch the pixie flit ahead of you, glancing back occasionally. You follow it among the trees for a long time. "I wonder if we should have trusted him," mutters Jay. "He may be leading us deeper into the woods!"

But then the pixie points between two trees. "Here's the way out," it calls.

You hurry between the trees—and find yourselves in a tiny glade surrounded by a thick wall of brambles. There is absolutely no way out except the way you came in.

You turn to scold the pixie for playing such a mean trick, but your blood runs cold at what you see. Standing between the two trees is a huge, shaggy creature that seems to be a cross between a bear and a bird of prey. It glares at you with red-rimmed eyes and licks its sharp, curved beak with a long pink tongue.

"Meet my pet owlbear," says the pixie from a branch high overhead. "I call it 'Daisy.' "

In rage you shout, "You promised to show us the way out!"

"No," says the pixie. "I promised that if you followed me, your troubles would soon be over." It giggles. "And they will be, as soon as Daisy has you for a midmorning snack!"

You begin a scream that is never completed as the owlbear lurches toward you. . . .

THE END

Without giving Jay a chance to say anything, you march straight up the stairs and knock loudly on the door.

After a short wait, the door creaks open, and you are relieved to see an elderly, harmless-looking bearded man dressed in a long robe of red velvet. In one hand, he holds a candle, which he lifts so that its light falls on the two of you. "What can I do for you two youngsters?" he asks pleasantly as he looks you over.

"We were hoping we could spend the night inside your tower, sir," you say. "We'll gladly sleep on the floor or anyplace. We just don't want to be outside at night."

"A wise decision," says the man. "Evil things roam at night hereabouts. Come in, by all means. I'm glad to have the company. However, just on the unlikely chance that you're thieves or robbers, I'd better tell you that I'm a wizard. Rogaldo is my name."

"Oh, we're not thieves," you assure him as you enter. "We're jugglers!" You pull out the three colored balls you carry with you and demonstrate your act for a moment.

"Very good!" he says with a grin. "But what are a pair of jugglers doing in an out-of-the-way place like this?"

"We're trying to get across the river," says Jay. "We're trying to find a town called Riverbend."

"Riverbend? That's quite a ways from here. You'll have to cross some dangerous territory to get there," Rogaldo says thoughtfully. "I hope it's important!"

"Very important! We promised to bury a man's bones," you blurt without thinking.

The wizard studies you both for a few moments, almost as if he is reading your faces. "I sense that you are on a quest," he says at last. "If so, I could go with you. Where there's a quest, there's usually treasure, and where there is treasure, there are often valuable magical things—spell books, wands, amulets, and the like. I don't care about the treasure, but if I used my magic to help you keep out of trouble, would you be willing to let me accompany you and have any magical items that might be found with the treasure?"

You and Jay stare at him, perplexed that he has discovered your secret. You have no need for any magical items you may find, and it would be useful to have a wizard with you— but can you trust him? Even though he says he doesn't care about treasure, what is to stop him from taking it once you've found it? On the other hand, if you tell him he can't come with you, he might put you under a spell. What should you do?

1) If you decide you can't trust the wizard, turn to page 49.

2) If you decide to trust Rogaldo, turn to page 9.

You and Jay decide you'll be better off waiting to have Redbeard along to brave the dangers of the treasure cave. While you wait, you earn money by doing your juggling act at inns. Sometimes there's barely enough to keep you all fed. But in a month, Redbeard is hale again, and following the map, you all set out in search of the hidden cave.

At about noon on the second day of your journey, you locate the hill. You climb up to a rocky slope, where you discover a dark cave.

"This must be it," says Jay, a bit nervously. Redbeard lights the three torches you have brought and you each take one. Redbeard enters the cave first, torch in one hand and sword in the other. You and Jay follow, each with a torch and a spear. You go cautiously through a narrow, winding passageway. Rounding a corner, you come to a large cavern.

"What's that big net doing here?" you ask. There's a huge net of thick ropes stretched across the middle of the cavern.

"That doesn't look like a net," says Jay. "It looks like— It's a spiderweb!"

With an exclamation, Redbeard raises his torch. And there, high on the web near the cavern roof, is a huge, hairy spider the size of a horse! This is what the man who gave you the map tried to warn you about!

The three of you stare aghast at the horrible creature. It seems to stare back at you out of its six dull, black eyes, but it does not move.

"I wonder . . ." mutters Redbeard. Tucking

his sword under the arm holding the torch, he bends down and picks up a rock off the floor. "Get ready to use your spears," he says, then throws the rock with all his might at the spider's head. The rock strikes one of the creature's eyes with a THUNK, but still the spider does not move.

"Luck is with us," says Redbeard. "It's dead!"

Then your eyes fall upon the pile of chests and bags behind the web. With your torch, you burn an opening in the web, and soon all the chests and bags are piled outside the cave. All that remains is to bury the bones of King Farad as you promised, then carry this treasure back to Riverbend—and be rich as kings for the rest of your lives!

THE END

"We—we'd love to have you come with us, sir, but—uh—" you stammer foolishly, trying to find a good reason for turning Rogaldo down.

"But you don't quite trust me, eh?" the wizard finishes for you, smiling slightly. "Well, I guess I can't blame you. But allow me to show you something."

You and Jay follow him sheepishly up a flight of stone stairs to a massive wooden door. Rogaldo unlocks the door, swings it open, and points inside. You peer into the room, and your eyes nearly pop with astonishment. The room is filled with treasure—mounds of gold and silver coins, cups, and dishes; chests of shimmering jewels; lumps of jade, ivory, ebony, and amber!

"So you see, I really don't need any more treasure," Rogaldo says, closing the door. "I have enough to buy anything I want or need for the rest of my life, so I have no interest in stealing your treasure. But magical items would be very useful to me. Now, I ask you once more: May I accompany you on your quest?"

"Yes," you and Jay blurt out together.

"Fine," Rogaldo says, smiling. "Now then, let me take you to a room where you can rest from your journey, then bright and early tomorrow, we'll set out for Riverbend."

Please turn to page 9.

You know that frogs usually don't snap at anything that isn't moving, so you decide to keep still.

You stay crouched, trying not to move a muscle or even breathe too loudly as the raft slides painfully slowly past the rows of goggle-eyed giants. Just in case, you have your hand on the hilt of your knife. Its short blade won't be much use against one of the huge creatures, but it somehow makes you feel a little safer to hold it.

Suddenly one of the frogs leans forward and opens its mouth. Its tongue, as long and thick as a boa constrictor, snaps out and wraps around you! You yell in fear as you realize that you're stuck to the tongue, like a fly on flypaper, and the frog is trying to pull you into its mouth!

Luckily your knife hand is free, and you flail out wildly, slashing at the thick snakelike tongue. The frog lets out a bellow of pain and releases you with such violence that you knock Jay off the raft into the water. The air seems filled with pale, leaping shapes as the frogs, frightened by the commotion, jump off in all directions.

Fortunately you're not far from the bank. You wade up onto it, Jay beside you, and crouch among the bulrushes and cattails, shivering in your wet clothes .

"That was too close for comfort!" you exclaim. "That frog was trying to eat me!"

"You were lucky to get out of that alive,

Sparrow!" Jay says, glancing about. "We'd better get out of here fast, Sparrow. If we follow the river, we'll get to Riverbend sooner or later, but we might run into more frogs—or something even worse—if we stay by the riverbank."

He points off to the right. "I'm pretty sure the road is off that way, but it may be miles from here, and who knows what kind of country there is between us and it? What shall we do, Sparrow—head for the road or stay by the river?"

1) If you choose to head toward the road, turn to page 129.

2) If you choose to follow the river, turn to page 13.

"I think we can trust Rogaldo, Jay," you say slowly. "He probably could have put us under a spell and taken the map for himself any time he wanted to, but he didn't. Let's wait until he's ready to go with us to look for the treasure cave. We may need him!"

The next morning Rogaldo shows up, ready to go but complaining of a headache. "I drank too much wine talking over old times with my friend, the wizard Vuverain," he groans.

Following the map, you head out into the hills beyond Riverbend. By late afternoon, you are climbing the hill that is marked on the map. Near the rocky summit, you find a dark opening in the hillside—the treasure cave!

"Stay close behind me," urges Rogaldo. "There may be all sorts of deadly dangers in there. Let's go!" As the three of you enter the cave, you notice that the tip of his wizard's staff begins to glow with a bright yellow light.

You make your way cautiously along a narrow, rocky passage until you come to a corner. Rogaldo slides around it slowly, holding his staff out in front of him, and you and Jay follow. You find yourselves in a large chamber. Rogaldo moves about cautiously, casting light into every corner. You see no tunnel or passageway leading out from the chamber, and there is no sign of any treasure.

"There's nothing here!" you exclaim, bitterly disappointed.

Rogaldo looks about grimly. "Something is wrong here," he announces. "This place reeks of magic—and done recently!" He points to a black, sooty smear on the cave floor. "Wizard's fire—perhaps used against whatever it was that the man who gave you the map tried to warn you of. I think someone destroyed it and took the treasure!"

You and Jay stare at each other in shock. "Who could have done it? No one knew about the treasure but us!" wails Jay.

"I may have the answer," Rogaldo says slowly, "but I have to get back to town to use some things I left in our room."

It's night by the time you reach Riverbend. You and Jay are gloomy and depressed. It seems as if your hopes and the promise you made to the dying man in the forest have been shattered. Silently you crawl into your beds in the room at the inn, while Rogaldo goes off with some magical tools he brought along.

It's still dark out when you are suddenly awakened. Rogaldo storms into the room, wild with anger.

"I found out by using my crystal ball," he snarls. "It was that rogue Vuverain! He got me drunk enough to talk about your quest and the cave, and somehow he must have managed to locate the cave magically. I saw him clearly, fleeing with the treasure, but he'll never get away with it! I'll follow him to the ends of the earth to pay him back for this!"

You and Jay leap from your beds and start pulling on your clothes. "We'll go with you!" you cry.

"Wait! It's not that easy," says the wizard grimly. "Vuverain is no fool. He took steps to guard against our following him. He's created an illusion of himself to mislead us."

"What do you mean?" you ask, confused.

"In the crystal ball, I saw two Vuverains, one heading north and one heading south," Rogaldo explains. "The two are exactly alike, and there's no way to tell which is the real one. If we follow the wrong one, we could lose track of the real Vuverain and never be able to find him or the treasure!"

He glances quickly from you to Jay. "Do either of you have any ideas? Your guess is as good as mine. Do we go north or go south?"

1) If you decide to go north, turn to page 133.

2) If you decide to go south, turn to page 93.

You're a good swimmer, and you think you'll have a chance in the river—it doesn't look dangerous. But if you try to bargain with the scarfaced man, offering the map for your life, he may just kill you whatever happens. And even if he doesn't, you'll have lost everything you and Redbeard have risked your lives for. You decide you have to try to keep the map out of Scarface's hands. You'll risk the river!

Taking a deep breath, you climb up on the rail quickly and dive headfirst into the river. Staying underwater as long as you can, you swim in the direction you think will take you under the far end of the bridge. When you're just about out of breath, you finally come to the surface. Perfect! You're right under the bridge, hidden by its shadow, and you're close to one of the wooden pilings that supports the bridge. You swim over and hide behind it.

"That cursed kid! I'll cut his nose off when I get my hands on him!" you hear Scarface howl.

"Where is he? I haven't seen him come up yet," yells one of the men.

You wait and wait and wait. Finally, when it seems as if an hour must surely have gone by, you swim to the bank and clamber up alongside the bridge. You peer cautiously from behind a railing. There's no one on the bridge. Scarface and his gang are gone!

"Sparrow! Sparrow!"

You turn toward the voice and see Jay! He rushes toward you and hugs you excitedly.

"I saw those men try to grab you," he says. "I was going to try to help, but then you dived into the river. They watched for you to come up for a while, and when you didn't, they finally left. But I knew you hadn't drowned. I figured you were just hiding somewhere."

"They wounded my friend Redbeard," you tell him. "Let's go see if we can help him."

You rush across the bridge to where Redbeard lies. His face is pale, his eyes are closed, and his leather jacket is bloodstained, but he is still breathing.

"Help me get him into town, Jay," you urge. "We've got to get him to a doctor! He saved my life earlier! We'll have to wait for him to get well so he can help us find the king's bones and the treasure."

Jay shakes his head. "He's hurt bad, Sparrow. He's going to need a lot of care—and it's going to cost a lot of money. I think you and I should go for the treasure ourselves as soon as possible. We're going to need it to help pay for your friend's care."

Jay is probably right, you realize. But do you dare seek the cave and its unknown dangers without the brave Redbeard there to help?

1) If you decide you must go without Redbeard, turn to page 111.

2) If you decide to wait until Redbeard is well again, turn to page 46.

You feel sure these warriors will understand the importance of your quest and won't be offended if you decide not to go see their king. You shake your head, and Jay gives a quick nod to show he agrees with you. He turns to the warrior. "We thank you for your offer," he tells him, "and we hope you won't be offended, but we really think we must refuse. We made a promise to bury the bones of a king, and we were journeying to do that when the goblins captured us. The king's spirit will not be at rest until his remains are safely buried."

The warrior nods slowly. "It is indeed an important thing you have to do. I agree you should resume your journey at once." He points toward a distant ridge. "Head for that hill. The river is just beyond it. But don't swim in the river. There are . . . 'things' in the water!"

You thank him for rescuing you and start out toward the hill. It's late afternoon when you reach it and nearly evening by the time you have climbed it and made your way down to the other side. Finally there before you is the river, much wider and deeper here than it was earlier.

"How do we get across?" Jay asks. "I don't see any bridge."

Just then something among the tall bulrushes lining the riverbank catches your eye. You dart down the bank, pushing the plants aside. Sure enough, there's a raft wedged among the thick growth! It's made of young saplings lashed together with leather thongs, and it's big enough to hold both of you.

"Look, Jay!" you call excitedly. "It's a raft! We don't have to walk anymore. We can float down the river all the way to Riverbend!"

Jay approaches and looks at the raft. "I don't know, Sparrow. I don't like the idea of taking something that doesn't belong to us," he says doubtfully. "That's stealing!"

"But there's not a house in sight, Jay," you point out. "There's no one around for it to belong to! I think it floated down the river and just got stuck here."

"You're probably right," Jay says dubiously, then shakes his head. "I still don't think it's a good idea. That warrior warned us there was something dangerous in this river. I don't think we'd be safe on this flimsy raft. I think we should just walk along the riverbank until we find a bridge."

1) If you decide to keep walking and look for a bridge, turn to page 140.

2) If you decide to take the raft down the river, turn to page 79.

You'd like nothing better than to get out of the Haunted Vale as quickly as possible, but you're afraid Redbeard might be disappointed in you. "Let's look for the lair!" you gulp.

"Good for you, lad!" says Redbeard. He picks up some of the tattered rags, then steps over to a nearby bush and hacks off a thick branch. "We'll need a torch," he says, wrapping the rags thickly around the end of the branch.

"Where should we look?" you ask.

"Well, the wight came from this way," says Redbeard, pointing. "Stay close to me, now."

He doesn't have to tell you that. The two of you hurry toward the foot of one of the hills that form one side of the vale.

"Look there!" you whisper. "That patch of dark shadow—is that a hole in the hillside?"

"It's an entrance, all right," says Redbeard. "Let me light this torch and we'll take a look."

After a moment, you hear the sound of flint striking steel. You peer about anxiously, making sure no other ghostly creature is trying to sneak up on you. When you look back at Redbeard, the torch is flaring and emitting nasty-smelling smoke from the burning rags.

"Let's go," says Redbeard. "But take care— no telling what's in here!" With the torch held high in one hand and his sword gripped in the other, he moves into the opening, with you pressing at his heels.

You wind your way through a short tunnel, then enter a large chamber. It seems to be empty except for several piles of bones. Beside one of the piles is a wooden chest, so old it is falling apart—and you can see gleams of gold and silver in the torchlight!

Suddenly you see something scuttle out of the shadows in a corner! It looks like a gigantic caterpillar with tentacles. Its body is a sickly, pale green color. The torchlight gleams off its bulging, glassy eyes.

"Move back, Sparrow!" shouts Redbeard.

You dodge as the creature lunges toward you, its tentacles writhing. Redbeard brings his sword down in a tremendous slash that slices right through the creature's body. There is a shower of green blood, then the two halves of the creature lie still.

"A carrion crawler!" says Redbeard disgustedly. "Good thing you avoided its tentacles. Their poison paralyzes their prey. Luckily for us, this one wasn't full-grown. Let's see what's in the chest and get out of here!"

With a kick, he breaks open the wooden chest. Two swords, two coats of silvery mail, and a mass of gold coins clatter onto the floor.

"Quick! Slip on a coat of mail, grab a sword, fill your pouch with coins, and let's go!" urges Redbeard.

You hasten to do as he says, and in moments you are both hurrying back up the tunnel. At the entrance, Redbeard turns and pitches the torch back inside. As it lies flaring in the tunnel, you can see in the shadows just beyond it the eyes of a huge carrion crawler!

"It won't come out here," Redbeard assures

you as you hurry down the hill. "We were lucky, Sparrow—these are magic swords and magical coats of mail or I'm a dragon! And we've got enough gold coins to make life easy for a couple of years!"

"What do we do now?" you ask.

"Well, the vale ends not far from here. Another mile after that, we'll come to the river. There's a ford there. We cross the ford, turn right, and we should be in Riverbend by noon tomorrow. On the other hand, if we turn to the right now, we could be back on the road in a few hours, and we'd be crossing the bridge into Riverbend by early morning."

He pauses a moment, then continues. "The only thing is, our friend Scarface and his creatures must have discovered our trick by now, and they may have decided to ride to the bridge and wait for us there."

For a moment, you ponder what to do. The ford seems safer, but Jay might be watching for you at the bridge. If you go into town by a different way, you might miss him, and he might start back up the road to search for you. Should you take the safer way and risk missing Jay, or should you head for the bridge and risk meeting Scarface and his crew?

1) If you decide to cross the ford, turn to page 25.

2) If you decide to head for the bridge, turn to page 127.

You look straight at Rogaldo. "I can't speak for Jay, but I think we ought to accept Vuverain's offer. We'll still be able to bury King Silverhair's bones as we promised, and we'll have enough treasure to make us rich—you, too, Rogaldo, if you decide to take a share after all. I think it's a lot better than fighting that duel and maybe having you get killed!"

"I agree with Sparrow," Jay says. "And we'll gladly share the treasure with you, Rogaldo."

Rogaldo smiles. "No, I still don't want any of your treasure. But I see your point. Why risk death for a whole cake when half a cake is plenty and won't cost anything? In a way, I suppose Vuverain did us a favor—he must have had to face whatever danger there was in the cave." He turns to Vuverain and shouts, "All right, Vuverain! We'll accept your offer for half the treasure!"

Vuverain draws a dagger and cuts the ropes of two of the horses. "These two are carrying a good half," he says and points toward one. "This one has King Silverhair's bones." Then he turns his horse and gallops off, leading his remaining two packhorses.

Rogaldo dismounts and says, "Come on, Sparrow, Jay. I'll help you bury the king. Your quest is over, and it's a lot better ending than it might have been!"

THE END

If the dragon is unfriendly, it will attack anyway. But even if it's friendly, if Rogaldo tries to blast it, it will also attack, you reason. "Wait and see if it's friendly," you urge. "That's our best chance!"

You wait tensely as the gigantic reptile draws so close you can see its gleaming eyes and brass-colored scales. If it plans to attack now, you are doomed.

You sigh with relief as the dragon comes to a landing about thirty paces in front of you. "Let us talk," it suggests in a surprisingly squawky voice.

Rogaldo does most of the talking for your group, although once in a while the dragon asks a question directly of you or Jay. The dragon reminds you in some ways of a very young child—full of questions about all sorts of things.

Finally it seems to have had enough, and it spreads its wings and takes off straight over your heads.

"It's a good thing we waited instead of trying to fight it," Rogaldo says. "We've only lost an hour of time—a fair price for our lives! Well, let's be off!"

Soon you are out of the desert, and you find yourself marching across a great plain. Before long, the narrow road intersects with a wider one, and you turn and follow the wide road. By nightfall you are in Riverbend. You and Jay rejoice that your quest is nearly over.

But that night your hopes for a speedy completion receive a surprising setback. At the inn where you have supper, Rogaldo meets an old friend, another wizard, named Vuverain. After conversing with his friend for some time, Rogaldo goes off with him, telling you he will see you in a day or so. You can hardly believe he would delay your quest with the end so near!

"I don't want to wait another day or so!" Jay tells you angrily. He rubs his chin and frowns with thought. "I wonder if we should still trust Rogaldo, Sparrow. What if he and his wizard friend locate the cave and decide to split the treasure between themselves? I think we should go out first thing in the morning and find that cave ourselves!"

You want to finish the quest right away, too, but you wonder if you shouldn't wait until Rogaldo is ready to come with you. He has been helpful so far, and you may well need his help even more when you reach the cave. Should you wait for him? Can he be trusted?

1) If you want to finish the quest by yourselves, turn to page 114.

2) If you want to wait for Rogaldo, turn to page 53.

"Jay, you've always done what you thought was best for me, and you've usually been right," you tell your brother. "But this time I want you to do what I think is best. I think we should try to finish this quest. We promised that dying man that we would!"

Jay nods. "All right, Sparrow," he says slowly, "if that's what you want."

Next morning, on horses bought with some of the wight's gold, the three of you set out. The map leads you in and out among the wild, desolate hilly land beyond Riverbend. Finally you come to the hill the map seems to indicate.

You tie the horses to a tree at the foot of the hill and start up the narrow, overgrown trail that leads to the hilltop. You and Redbeard have your magic swords and Jay carries a spear.

Halfway to the top, Redbeard suddenly stops dead. "Don't move!" he hisses in a low voice. "And don't get excited. Above all, don't act like you want to fight."

"What's the matter?" exclaims Jay.

"We're surrounded!" says Redbeard.

Looking around, you see, half-hidden behind bushes and peering out from behind boulders, an unknown number of strange-looking men. Their forms are short and stocky, with long, shaggy hair and broad faces. Armed with spears that have points made out of sharp pieces of stone, they wear no clothes except for ragged pieces of animal skin tied around their waists.

"Who—who are they?" you whisper.

"Cavemen," answers Redbeard. "They're human but very primitive. They usually stay away from our kind, and they aren't dangerous unless you get too close to where they live. I'm afraid that's what we've done."

"Uh-oh!" you exclaim. "You think they're living in the treasure cave?"

"I suspect so," Redbeard says, sheathing his sword. "Luckily I've had dealing with cavemen before. I speak their language a little. I'll see if I can find out how things stand."

Slowly raising his hands to show he has no weapons, Redbeard calls out a few words in a growly-sounding language. One of the cavemen steps out of hiding and answers him. A short conversation follows.

Turning back to you and Jay, Redbeard says, "They want to know why we have come here, and I told them we're seeking a cave that holds something that belongs to us. They want us to meet with their chief. The cave is their home, all right, and they're afraid we mean it harm."

You start up the trail again, this time with cavemen on each side of you. "What do you think they'll do to us?" you ask nervously.

"I don't know," says Redbeard, "but if things look too bad, I can always challenge their chief to combat. If I win, I become chief!"

"Yes, but what if you lose?" you think.

Near the crest of the hill, you see a broad, rocky ledge and the dark opening of a cave.

Grouped before it are all the cave people—
men, women, and naked little children, staring at you with wide eyes. One of the men
steps forward and says something.

"This is their chief," says Redbeard. You certainly hope Redbeard DOESN'T have to fight
him, because he's just as tall as Redbeard and
has muscles like a bull!

The chief and Redbeard speak together for a
long time. Finally Redbeard turns to you and
Jay.

"He says the cave is sacred to them and we
can't go inside. They had to kill a giant spider
that was living in the cave before they could
move in. He says there was also some stuff in
the cave that they've just left there—bags and
boxes of shiny, flat round things and sparkly
stones."

"The treasure!" Jay exclaims.

"What about King Farad's bones?" you ask
anxiously.

Redbeard questions the chief a moment,
then turns back to you once more. "He says
there were some old bones in a bag, but they
buried them so the ghost wouldn't be troubled
anymore," says Redbeard.

You're glad that king Farad has been put to
rest at last, but somehow you wish you and
Jay could have been the ones to do it. It looks
as if the quest is going to end without accom-
plishing any of the things you set out to do.

The chief says something else to Redbeard.
Redbeard turns to you, and you can see that he

is struggling to keep from breaking into a grin. "The chief says that the children sometimes play with the shiny stuff in the cave, but it isn't good for anything else. He says if that is what we want, he'll trade it to us for something useful!"

Now it's your turn to struggle to keep from grinning. You don't want to let the chief see just how much you want that 'junk'!

"But what can we trade them?" asks Jay. "We don't have anything to trade."

"They want our weapons," says Redbeard. "Your spear, Jay, and my and Sparrow's swords. THOSE are treasures for these people." He takes out his sword and looks at it. "This magic sword has come in mighty handy, but I have a feeling that with my share of the treasure, I can retire and never have to lift a sword again. What about you, Sparrow? Are you willing to part with your magic sword?"

"Yes!" you answer emphatically. You feel you've had enough excitement to last a lifetime.

That afternoon, the three of you head back to Riverbend, your horses loaded with bags and boxes of coins and jewels.

"I'd say things turned out pretty well," booms Redbeard. "King Farad is at rest, all of us are as rich as lords, and even the cavemen are happy. What more could you ask from a quest?"

THE END

"Let's cross the ford, Redbeard," you suggest. "The story about the nixie is probably just a rumor. But if we run into Scarface and his gang, we'll be in real trouble!"

You reach the river in less than an hour. You both remove your shoes and wade into the water. Even at midstream it's no higher than your knees in this part of the river.

But as you reach the middle of the stream, you stop suddenly. Somehow you just don't want to go on. A strange numbness has come over you, as if you are dreaming. Hazily you notice that Redbeard, too, has stopped.

You turn, as if obeying a command. Off to your right, in deeper water, stands a strange figure, like a man but with a pale green scaly body, webbed hands, and staring, fishlike eyes. It is a nixie—and though you realize it has cast its spell over you, that somehow doesn't seem to matter.

The nixie beckons, and you and Redbeard follow it into the deeper part of the river until the water closes over your heads. You're not even surprised to find you can breathe underwater as the creature leads you down to the bottom of the river.

Now begins a strange life. You move about in the nixie's underwater palace, doing the creature's bidding without thinking or feeling. You feel no sensation of days or nights, weeks, months, or years.

Finally, when it seems as if you have lived your whole life in this strange place, the nixie

apparently grows bored with you. It takes you by the hand and leads you up out of the water to the riverbank. As you step onto shore, the nixie vanishes back into the water. You are free!

Suddenly you remember everything just as if it is the day you were captured. You recall the quest, Jay, Redbeard, Riverbend. You gasp in dismay as you wonder how long you've been beneath the river. Your clothes seem too tight, and your arms and legs look bigger than they should be. You reach up to scratch your chin and feel a fuzzy beard! You've grown up! You must have been the nixie's slave for years!

Anxiously you fumble at your belt pouch and remove the parchment on which the map was drawn. It is nothing but a soggy lump, without a mark on it! The long soaking in the water has washed it clean!

You know now you will never be able to locate the treasure or the bones of King Silverhair. You have no idea where Redbeard is, or for that matter, Jay either. He probably gave you up for dead long ago.

With a heavy heart, you start trudging toward Riverbend. Just MAYBE you'll find Jay or Redbeard there, if the nixie has let Redbeard go, too. Just MAYBE you'll somehow be able to find the treasure, if you can remember enough about the map. But maybe you won't. . . .

THE END

In panic, you turn and dash into the heart of the marsh. If you can just get away from the dinosaur, maybe you'll be able to find your way back to the path later. But even if you lose your way, at least you'll be alive and not in the giant reptile's belly! You wish you knew where Redbeard was, but he's nowhere in sight. You hope he's all right!

You flounder through the cattails and bulrushes until you're out of breath. You crouch down among the tall plants, panting. When you regain your breath again, you decide to stay where you are. You feel safe and hidden, and you are so tired that, after a time, you actually lie down and fall asleep.

Sometime later, you waken with a start. You realize you've been lucky no marsh monsters came upon you while you were asleep! Cautiously you stand up and look around. The marsh is one vast sea of tall plant stems, and you have no idea which way the road lies. But you can't just stay here—you've got to find the way out.

The sky is slowly turning pink now as the sun rises. The sounds of the marsh creatures are dying out. Perhaps they sleep during the day. If so, that could mean less chance of running into a monster—although there's still the danger of stepping into quicksand.

The sun rises higher and you wander on. Soon it's full daylight, and you feel as if you've been tramping for hours. You still can't see anything but an endless expanse of tall plants on all sides. There MUST be an end to this awful place! But you're beginning to fear that you could wander about until you die of hunger or thirst—or until some monster gets you!

By midafternoon, you're feeling the effects of the sun beating down on you for hours. You gaze longingly at some of the shallow pools of water you pass, wondering if it would be safe to drink from them. But when you peer closely into one, you see that it's full of tiny wriggly things.

On and on you trudge, growing hotter and more thirsty every minute. You almost wish you COULD die and get it over with! Then, abruptly, you push your way through a clump of tall plants and find yourself looking at a river!

Whooping with joy, you race to the bank and fling yourself down to take a long drink. Then you splash water over your head to cool off. It feels great!

You know that the dangers of the marsh are behind you now, and your spirits start to rise. You're pretty sure this must be the river that's on your map. If it is, all you have to do is follow it, and you'll eventually get to Riverbend. You won't have to worry about being thirsty, and you can eat fish, if you're able to catch some. You'll survive!

Rising to your feet, you glance up the river, and you freeze with astonishment. Far in the distance, there is a small boat coming toward you. Maybe you can get a ride to Riverbend!

You wait for the boat to come nearer. Soon you can make out that it is a raft, with one person guiding it along with a pole. With growing amazement, you stare until the raft is close enough for there to be no doubt. Then you let out a whoop of joy—the person on the raft is your brother Jay!

Jay quickly poles the raft to shore and in moments the two of you are hugging and pounding each other on the back.

"How did you find the river?" you ask.

"I was lost in the woods for a long time," Jay explains. "I just wandered until suddenly I came to a river. There were lots of logs and vines around, so I built this raft and let the river take me out. I've been floating down-river ever since. How did YOU get here?"

Eagerly you tell him about your adventures. By the time you finish, your stomach is growling. "I'm awfully hungry, Jay. I haven't eaten a thing since last night!"

Jay opens his belt pouch and takes out the fish hooks and line he always carries. The two of you fish for a while and finally catch a large trout, which you cook over a campfire.

You notice it's nearly dark again. The sounds of the marsh are starting up once more. "We don't dare camp here, Jay," you tell him. "This is an awfully dangerous place. We'd be safer on the raft."

"Let's climb aboard, then," Jay says.

Please turn to page 79.

You push off from shore, and once the raft is floating smoothly, you and Jay stretch out side by side. As you lie there looking up at a sky aglow with stars and a full moon, your eyes gradually close, and before long you drift off to sleep.

You are awakened by a pressure on your arm and the sound of Jay excitedly whispering your name. "Huh? What's the matter?" you mumble, still half asleep.

"Shh! Don't make any noise. Take a look around!"

Sleepily you glance off to one side, and suddenly your eyes snap wide open. The raft is drifting on a narrow part of the stream, with the banks no more than several arm lengths away on each side. In the bright moonlight, you can see clearly that both banks are lined with scores of huge, silent, crouching shapes. You realize with a shudder that the shapes you see are gigantic frogs, nearly three times the size of a man! Their bodies are dark green, with yellow blotches, and their huge, pale, bulging eyes gleam faintly as they stare at you.

"What are we going to do now, Jay?" you whisper.

"I don't know," Jay whispers back. "Maybe if we just try to lie still, they won't bother us, and we can drift on past them. But they might attack anyway! Maybe we should yell and see if we can scare them away. What do you think, Sparrow?"

1) If you decide to try to frighten the frogs away, turn to page 135.

2) If you decide to lie still and try to drift by the frogs, turn to page 50.

Your life has been in almost constant danger in the last few days—from wolves in the woods, a wight, a carrion crawler, and a nixie. Now you're being asked to risk your life yet again against Scarface and his band of cutthroats, who outnumber your group two to one. It seems as if you've risked your life enough!

But the more you think about it, the angrier you get that Scarface has stolen the map and ruined your quest after all the risks you've taken. Well, you're not going to let him get away with it without a fight! You slam your fist down on the table and exclaim, "We're going after them!" Redbeard grins broadly and slaps you on the back.

Next morning, at sunrise, you and Redbeard are lying on the top of a hill that looks down upon the road leading out of Riverbend. Behind you, out of sight, Jay holds the three horses you bought last night. He clutches a stout spear.

"Here they come!" whispers Redbeard.

You squint your eyes and see six horsemen, tiny at this distance, riding out of town. You watch as they pass beneath you and head off into the hills. When they are nearly out of sight, they come to a fork in the road and take the path to the right.

"All right, we know which way they're headed," says Redbeard, scrambling to his feet.

You hurry to the horses, mount, and ride

down the hillside to the road. In a few minutes, you reach the fork and follow the same path Scarface's band took. All morning you trot along, following the prints of horses' hooves in the soft dirt of the road. It's nearly noon when Redbeard pulls up his horse and leans down to look carefully at the hoofprints.

"They turned off the road here," he reports. "They went up this hill. We'd better dismount and walk the horses up to keep the noise down."

You lead your horses up the hillside as quietly as you can. The higher you go, the more rocky the hill becomes. Near the top, you see the dark, yawning mouth of a cave, and tethered to an old twisted tree stump nearby are six horses. There is no sign of the men.

"Keep the horses out of sight and lie low," suggests Redbeard. "We'll wait for them to come out of the cave, and then we'll rush them. You and I have our magic swords, Sparrow. That should help even things up!"

You don't have to wait long. Scarface and his two half-orc followers soon appear, dragging some chests and bags. After a time, you realize that the other three members of the gang aren't going to show up—something must have happened to them in the cave.

"Three to three—even up!" whispers Redbeard. "That puts things in our favor! I'll take Scarface and you each take an orc. Come on!"

You rush from hiding and sprint toward the

three bandits. Cursing, Scarface draws his sword and advances to meet you, the two half-orcs right behind him!

One of the orcs dodges around you and thrusts its sword at your chest. But to the orc's amazement—and yours—the blade merely bounces off you! Your coat of magic armor has saved you! You swing wildly with your sword, and the blade bites deep into the orc's arm. With a howl, it drops its sword and flees.

You hurry to help Jay, who is having trouble with the other orc. But when the creature sees it is outnumbered, it, too, flees.

You turn to see if Redbeard needs help, but he is standing over Scarface's lifeless body. The fight is over, and the treasure is yours!

But first, while Redbeard stands watch to see that the three others don't return, you and Jay bury the bag containing the bones of King Farad Silverhair. You have finally kept your promise to the stranger who gave you the map!

You load the treasure onto the spare horses and start back toward Riverbend. "I wonder what happened to Scarface's other three men inside the cave?" Jay asks after a time.

"I'd rather not know!" you exclaim. "We risked our lives enough times on this quest, but now the risks are over. We're all as rich as princes—and King Farad Silverhair can sleep in peace forever!"

THE END

You remember hearing people say, "Never trust a pixie," and decide there must be good reason for that advice.

"No, thank you," you tell the pixie. "We'll find the way out for ourselves."

"You'll be sorry! I hope you starve to death! I hope the wolves get you!" shrieks the pixie and vanishes from sight.

"Let's go this way," suggests Jay, pointing to the right. You begin to trudge through the trees. You hope you weren't wrong about the pixie, but it's too late now.

Soon you find yourselves on the bank of a sparkling stream. You both fling yourselves down for a long, cool drink, then fill your water flasks.

Suddenly Jay exclaims, "This is it, Sparrow! All we have to do is follow this stream, and it'll lead us out of the woods! In fact, unless I miss my guess, it'll lead us right to Riverbend. Come on. Let's go!"

But the stream has given you an idea, too. "Why don't we build a raft? There are plenty of logs and vines around. Then we can FLOAT to Riverbend."

"Great idea!" Jay exclaims. The two of you begin collecting logs and lashing them together with vines. It's noon by the time you finish. You step onto the raft and push off from shore, using two long poles made from tree branches.

It's pleasant floating down the stream in the shade of the leafy treetops overhead. By late afternoon, you see that the trees are thinning out, and before long you are out of the woods. The stream flows lazily through a broad, rolling plain.

You and Jay guide the raft to shore and pull it up onto the bank. In your travels, you have often camped beside rivers, so you both have fishhooks and line in your belt pouches. You spend some time fishing, and Jay finally lands a fine trout for supper.

After you've eaten, Jay says, "I wonder if we should spend the night here or get back on the raft. We could gain a lot of time floating along while we're asleep."

"But would it be safe?" you ask.

1) If you decide to spend the night right where you are, turn to page 142.

2) If you decide to sleep on the raft while you float downriver, turn to page 79.

After you think about it for a moment, it seems to you that the road would be far safer than the ford. You certainly have no desire to spend the rest of your life at the bottom of the river as the underwater slave of a nixie! Besides, Scarface and his gang surely must have given up watching for you by now.

"Let's take the road, Redbeard," you decide.

You travel the rest of the afternoon and reach the road late in the day. Just as you get to it, you see a large procession of people coming toward you, headed toward Riverbend. Some of them are carrying banners, some are singing, and some are chanting.

"Looks like a procession of pilgrims on their way to some religious shrine," comments Redbeard. "That gives me an idea, Sparrow. If Scarface and his crew are still looking for us, they won't expect to find us in a crowd. We could sort of join in with these pilgrims until we get to Riverbend."

As the pilgrims throng past you, Redbeard hails one of the men over to the side of the road. "Where are you headed, brother?"

"Why, to visit the shrine of the holy Swithian of Blofusk, of course," he answers cheerfully.

"Swithian of Blofusk!" cries Redbeard. "Ah, what a devout person he was! We'll join you." He tugs you by the arm. "Come on, Sparrow. Just smile a lot and don't say anything."

So here you are, marching along with a crowd of people heading for the shrine of

Swithian of Blosfusk, when you don't even
have the faintest idea who he is, or was. You'd
be willing to bet Redbeard doesn't, either.
However, no one pays much attention to you,
and as for Redbeard, he acts right at home pre-
tending to join in the singing and chanting
and even holding one of the banners for a
while!

Before too long, you see a wooden bridge in
the distance—the bridge that crosses the river
into Riverbend! But as you draw near, your
heart nearly jumps into your throat as you see
that Redbeard was right—Scarface and his
henchmen are standing at the near end of the
bridge!

Redbeard has seen them, too. He bends
down and whispers in your ear, "Keep your
head down and don't look toward them. If luck
is with us, they won't even notice us in this
crowd." Then he folds his arms across his chest
and covers his beard with one hand as if he is
pondering some deep thought.

With your head down and your eyes on your
feet, you shuffle slowly along, wishing you
could run instead! You can feel your heart
pounding. At any moment, you expect to be
seized by Scarface or one of his henchmen.
However, you're smaller than most of the people around you, so maybe you won't be seen
after all.

Before long you feel your feet thudding on
the wooden boards of the bridge, and after
what seems an eternity, you're walking on

cobblestones. You're across the bridge and in Riverbend!

Suddenly you feel someone seize you! You are pulled roughly out of the procession and into a side street, where Redbeard confronts you, grinning broadly. "We did it, Sparrow! The stupid ruffians never even noticed us! Well, now that we're here, what's next?"

"We have to try to find Jay," you tell him. "Let's go back and take a quick look from this side of the bridge. He may have been watching for me and didn't see me in the crowd."

You return to the bridge, staying well back in the crowd of spectators who have gathered to watch the pilgrims, and cautiously look around for Jay. But he's nowhere to be seen.

"Let's start asking at the inns," suggests Redbeard. "He'd have to stay somewhere while he was waiting for you to get here."

You go to every inn in town, describing Jay to every innkeeper, but no one has seen him.

"It looks as if he's not here yet," says Redbeard. "He might still show up today, but if he doesn't, what will we do, Sparrow? Do we keep waiting for him, or do we start out tomorrow for Farad's bones and the treasure and get it over with?"

1) If you decide to keep waiting for Jay, turn to page 97.

2) If you decide to finish the quest without Jay, turn to page 136.

You decide you must risk having a fire. Who knows what dangerous creatures might be lurking in a dark forest? When night comes, the forest turns completely black all around you. The orange glow of the fire comforts you, and after a while you grow sleepy, so you lie down beside the crackling fire and close your eyes.

"Wake up!" you hear a voice call. Someone is prodding you in the ribs.

Your eyes snap open. The fire is nearly out, but by its dim glow, you see that you are surrounded by a group of slim, light-haired men with pale eyes. They carry longbows and are dressed in garments of white and pale green. Elves!

"Humans are not permitted to leave the road and enter our forest," says one of them sternly. "Stand up!"

"We couldn't help it," says Jay as you scramble to your feet. "Bandits were after us, and we—"

"I do not care to hear your excuses," snaps the leader of the elves. "Search them!" he orders.

The others examine your water flask, peer into your food bag, and take the map from your belt pouch. The leader looks at it with growing interest. "This is a treasure map! Where did you get it?"

"A stranger gave it to us," you tell him.

"Bah! Why would anyone give away a treasure map!" he says angrily. "It's more likely you stole it. We shall keep it as a fine for breaking our law. Come with us."

There is nothing you can do but follow the elves through the forest. They take you back to the road, and the leader points toward the right. "That is the shortest way out of the forest. Be sure you are out of it before morning!" Then he and his companions vanish into the darkness.

"I guess we'll never be rich after all," you say sadly. "If the elves go after the treasure, I hope they bury poor King Silverhair's bones."

Jay claps you on the shoulder. "Cheer up, Sparrow. We're no worse off than we were when we started out through the forest. And we're still the world's best jugglers!"

Together you trudge through the darkness toward the end of the forest. "Jay's right," you think as you go. "We're no worse off than before. And who knows what might happen tomorrow?"

THE END

"Which way is south?" you ask suddenly. Rogaldo looks puzzled, then points toward the window. You glance toward Jay, whose right shoulder is facing the same window. "Right is right," you say. "We're going south!"

"When do we start?" Jay asks.

"The sooner the better," the wizard replies. "Vuverain is on horseback and has a full day's head start on us. We'll have to get some horses of our own to keep up with him. If he gets much farther ahead, I won't be able to keep an eye on him with my crystal ball. He'll have to stop sooner or later, and then we'll have him—unless we're following the illusion."

You manage to rouse a horse dealer, and Rogaldo buys three fast mounts. Then you begin a wild ride to catch up with Vuverain!

You ride steadily until sunrise and on through the whole morning. At noon, you stop for a quick meal, and Rogaldo consults his crystal ball. "We've gained on him," he announces. "His horses are loaded with stolen treasure and can't move very fast. And I don't think he has any idea that we're chasing him."

All afternoon you ride on, and well into the night. Finally you stop for a few hours of sleep. Checking the crystal ball again, Rogaldo sees that Vuverain has also stopped to rest.

"Well, at least we know he won't gain on us during the night," observes Jay.

"Yes, and more important, it also proves that we're following the real Vuverain,"

Rogaldo says with satisfaction. "The illusion wouldn't have needed to rest!"

You've been worried that your hunch might prove wrong, but now that you know the real Vuverain is ahead of you, you begin to feel that the quest may turn out all right after all.

You start off again at dawn. Once more you rest only briefly during the day. At nightfall, Rogaldo says that you should catch up with him tomorrow!

Morning dawns gray and drizzling. You gallop on, unmindful of your aching muscles, and by noon, you can actually see Vuverain and his horses far in the distance.

Now Vuverain knows you're behind him. He tries to speed his horses along, but they are loaded too heavily. The distance between you gets shorter and shorter.

Suddenly you see Vuverain bring his horses to a halt. He faces you with one hand raised.

"He wants to talk," grunts Rogaldo. "I think he wants to make some kind of a deal."

You slow down and pull your horses to a stop some hundred paces from the enemy wizard. You get your first good look at Vuverain, a tall, thin man with piercing black eyes, a beaklike nose, and a scraggly black beard.

"Say what you have to say, Vuverain!" Rogaldo calls coldly.

"Just this," comes the reply. "There's enough treasure here to share. I'll make you an offer—the king's bones and half the treasure in return for calling off the chase."

"What if we don't agree to that?" Rogaldo calls back.

"Then I challenge your honor as a wizard to fight me in a wizard's duel, Rogaldo. If I win, I get to keep everything for myself!"

"What's a wizard's duel?" you ask.

"A magical combat—to the death!" Rogaldo explains. "Each wizard assumes the form of any kind of living creature and then tries to kill his opponent. The only rules are that you must become only living things, and you can't turn into any one thing more than once."

"It sounds dangerous!" Jay says.

"It is. You have to know the strengths and weaknesses of every living thing. Make one wrong guess and you're dead!"

You glance at Jay and know he's thinking the same thing you are. It might be better to settle for King Silverhair's bones and half the treasure than let Rogaldo risk his life. But the fierce expression on Rogaldo's face seems to indicate he wants to fight the other wizard. Should you try to talk him out of fighting Vuverain or let him do it?

1) If you choose to accept Vuverain's offer of half the treasure and King Silverhair's bones in return for letting Vuverain get away, turn to page 65.

2) If you elect to let Rogaldo fight Vuverain to the death in a wizard's duel, turn to page 154.

"I can hardly stand not to go on after the treasure when we're so close to it now," you tell Redbeard, "but I just have to wait for Jay. We promised to go on the quest together. Jay would be terribly hurt if I went ahead and finished it without him. I have to wait for him at least a few more days, Redbeard!"

Redbeard says nothing, but you feel that he understands.

By pooling small amounts of money you're able to take a room at an inn for a few days. You go to bed that night hoping Jay will arrive tomorrow.

You awaken to see morning sunlight streaming in through the window. After a yawn and a stretch, you roll out of bed to wash up. Suddenly you notice that Redbeard's bed is empty. As you glance at it, you see there's a square of paper, covered with writing, lying on the pillow. You go to the bed and see that it is a note for you, and you read it curiously.

"Sparrow,
"I have the map. Please don't think I'm planning to cheat you, because I'm not. But your brother may not show up for a long time, and I just don't think we can afford to wait. I have gone to find the treasure, and I promise I'll bring it back. By that time, maybe Jay will be there and we'll all be able to celebrate together. Please trust me and don't be angry.
                                        "Redbeard"

Quickly you turn toward your clothing, which you left piled on a chair last night. It's true—the pouch with the map in it, which was tied to your belt, is gone!

You read the note over and over. You can't believe that Redbeard intends to cheat you, or he would simply have taken the map and not left a note. You must trust him, but still you are worried as you go to watch for Jay.

You go to the bridge to watch for Jay. You keep back well out of sight, because Scarface and his men are still watching on the other side.

The day passes with no sign of Jay. You return to the inn in the evening, hoping desperately that Redbeard will be there, but the room is empty. You find it hard to go to sleep because you're worried about Jay and Redbeard.

In the morning, you return to the bridge. Today you see no sign of Scarface and his gang. Apparently they have finally given up.

All morning you watch hopefully, but Jay never appears. It is almost noon when you notice, far in the distance, river, what appears to be a man on a raft coming down the river toward town. You watch as the raft approaches. Finally you let out a whoop of joy—it's Jay! You rush down the bank to the edge of the river, waving your arms to attract his attention.

Jay poles the raft to shore, and you hug and slap each other on the back. "How did you happen to come down the river? Where did you get the raft?" you ask excitedly.

"After we got separated, I got lost awhile in the woods," he explains. "Then I came to a river and realized the river could take me out. So I built the raft out of logs and vines, and here I am! But tell me how you got here."

Quickly you tell Jay about your adventures with Redbeard, and he listens with astonishment. But when he hears what Redbeard his done, his face grows sober. "Sparrow, I'm afraid you'll never see him again!"

"Redbeard wouldn't cheat me," you insist. "He may even be back at the inn right now."

But when you return to the inn, Redbeard is not there. Neither of you has any money, and this is the last day you can use the room at the inn. You explain to the innkeeper that you and Jay are jugglers, and he agrees to let you work at the inn in return for a room and whatever money the customers may give you.

So you begin to scratch out a meager living in Riverbend, and the days pass quickly. Finally you must admit to yourself that the quest is over and you have failed. You will never see Redbeard again. Either he found the treasure and decided to cheat you after all, or else he met some horrible death from whatever the danger was that the dying man in the woods tried to warn you of. But you will never know for sure what happened, and for you, this looks like . . .

THE END

You can't just run away and leave the red-bearded warrior to fight three enemies by himself! You must stay and help him however you can.

Redbeard fends off an attack by Scarface and one of the others, but the third attacker, a half-orc, circles stealthily around behind him. You grab a heavy pitcher from a table and hurl it with all your might at the orc's head. It smashes against the side of his face, and he staggers back in a daze, dropping his sword.

Meanwhile, Redbeard has run his sword through the arm of Scarface's other hench-man, putting him out of the fight, too. Cursing, Scarface backs out the door, dragging the wounded man with him. The half-orc staggers after them. Redbeard, bellowing with laughter, gives it a hearty kick in the rump that sends the creature sprawling through the door.

"Thanks for your help, lad," Redbeard says with a wink. "We showed them something, I'd say." He looks at you curiously. "Why were they after you, anyway?"

You hesitate briefly, then decide to trust this big, hearty man. After all, he befriended you the moment you entered the inn, then risked his life to save you from your enemies. Taking a deep breath, you tell him of your quest to bury the remains of Farad Silverhair and find the treasure. Then you explain why Scarface is pursuing you.

He whistles and eyes you with concern.

"You're in a bad spot, lad. As long as this Scar-face thinks you have the map, he'll keep after you—and I won't be around to help next time."

But his words give you an idea. "Why don't you join me and my brother?" you suggest. "We'll give you a third of whatever treasure we find."

He ponders thoughtfully for a moment, then grins and holds out his hand. "I accept your offer, lad. Braving danger to give rest to a troubled spirit is a worthy cause—and besides, I'm running a bit short on money. Come on—let's have some supper. By the way, call me Redbeard."

You grin, but you don't bother to tell him that's what you've been calling him all along in your thoughts.

Early next morning you start out together, following the road that leads to the distant town of Riverbend, where you hope your brother Jay may be waiting. From time to time, you glance back down the road on the chance you might see him coming along behind you. Once or twice you think you do see a figure or group of figures far in the distance, but you're not sure.

You travel all day. At twilight you stop, build a small campfire by the side of the road, and have a supper of bread and cheese.

"Listen, Sparrow," Redbeard says in a low voice, "I'm certain we're being followed. I sus-pect it's our scar-faced friend and his gang!"

"I thought I saw someone behind us today!"

you exclaim. "I'll bet they plan to wait until late at night, when we're asleep, then sneak up and kill us!" A sudden idea pops into your mind. "Listen, Redbeard, why don't we trick 'em? When it gets dark we'll leave the fire burning as if we're here, but we'll sneak off and hide out somewhere in the darkness!"

"A good plan," he says with a grin. "We can escape from them completely, Sparrow, because I know two shortcuts that will take us straight to the river we have to cross to get to Riverbend. Scarface and his cutthroats won't have any idea where we've gone!"

"Great!" you chuckle.

"There's something you ought to know first, though," he says, looking you square in the eye. "Neither shortcut is very safe. One goes through a marsh that has some very dangerous things in it. The other is through a vale that's said to be haunted. But either way is better than staying here and getting our throats cut, eh?"

"Right," you gulp, beginning to wonder.

"You make the choice, then," he says. "Which shall it be—the Haunted Vale or the Marsh of Monsters?"

1) If you choose to take the shortcut through the Haunted Vale, turn to page 37.

2) If you choose to travel through the Marsh of Monsters, turn to page 123.

The more you consider your idea to trick the giant, the more farfetched it seems. Redbeard is probably right. The only way to deal with the giant is to rush it while it's still asleep. You may not have another chance.

"Let's try rushing it," you whisper.

Redbeard nods and draws his sword. You level your spear.

"Now!" Redbeard whispers sharply. Side by side, you race toward the slumbering giant.

But you aren't halfway there when its eyes flash open and glare at you. With an angry roar, the giant leaps to its feet and lumbers toward you. You feel the breeze from its huge club as it whistles through the air and smashes into Redbeard's body. The force of the blow knocks Redbeard twenty feet, and when he strikes the ground, he lies motionless.

You haven't a chance and you know it. Dropping the spear, you turn to run. But the giant can cover twice as much ground with its huge strides as you can. In an instant, you hear its panting breath right behind you, and a huge shadow looms over you. The last thing you hear is the harsh SWISH of its club. . . .

THE END

Suddenly one of Jay's favorite sayings flashes into your mind: "When you're not sure which way to go, right is right!" On the chance that Jay will turn right, you swim for the right bank. You pull yourself up onto the muddy ground and glance fearfully behind you, but there's no sign of the monster now.

There's no sign of Jay, either. What if he swam to the other side after all? Then you hear his voice. "Sparrow! Are you there?"

"Here!" you answer, and in moments you're together again. Jay explains how he headed for the right bank, hoping you'd remember he'd do that. But when he didn't find you there, he remembered you were facing each other on the raft—his right was your left—so he swam back across the river. "That was a close call, Jay!" you exclaim.

"We've got to get away from this place fast! Let's follow the river and pray we don't meet any more monsters!"

You trudge along for what seems like several hours. You begin to feel awfully tired.

"I see something up ahead," Jay says finally. "It looks like a building of some sort."

You look up and see it, too—a tall, windowless tower about three floors high, made of stone. When you reach it, you find a flight of stone steps leading up to a small door.

"I'm going to knock and see if whoever lives here will let us spend the night," you say.

Please turn to page 44.

After talking it over, you and Jay decide that the longer journey will be worth it if you meet up with less danger.

The plain is an endless expanse of tall golden grass. You travel uneventfully for the rest of the day. At nightfall, you build a small fire and eat, with the sound of wolves howling in the distance. "The fire will keep them away," says Rogaldo. You hope so!

The next day you sight a herd of large shaggy creatures grazing in the distance. "Wild cattle," says Rogaldo. "They're no danger unless they should stampede."

Near noon of the third day, you come to a wild and desolate stretch. Huge boulders lie scattered about, and there are broad patches of bare ground. Suddenly, from among a cluster of boulders, a large round thing, wider than a man is tall, begins to float swiftly toward you!

"A beholder!" Rogaldo says fearfully.

Hardly daring to breathe, you examine the weird creature as it approaches. It has a single huge eye in its center and an enormous mouth filled with sharp teeth. From its top sprouts a cluster of stalks with smaller eyes on their tips. The thing floats to a stop near you and speaks in a strange language.

Rogaldo answers in the same language, then turns to you and Jay. "We may be in luck. These things usually attack on sight, but this one will let us pass if we pay it a bribe."

"Can you use magic on it?" you whisper.

"It can protect itself against any magic, plus it can do things that my magic can't stop," Rogaldo says grimly. "We must do as it wishes or it will destroy us! Quick! Show it everything you have!"

You hurriedly open all the bags and dump their contents onto the ground. The creature watches with its huge eye, then speaks.

"It wants to see what is in your pouch, Sparrow," Rogaldo interprets.

There is nothing in your pouch but the map. Trembling, you dump the map on the ground and spread it open. The beholder looks at it for a few moments, then speaks once more.

"It wants the map," says Rogaldo. "We have no choice. We must give it up or die!"

He picks up the map and holds it out. The beholder takes the parchment in its lips, then slowly floats back to its nest of boulders.

"Quick! Gather up what you can and let's get away from here," urges Rogaldo, hurriedly scooping things into bags. "We're lucky to still be alive!" He lowers his voice, glancing from you to Jay. "There's still a chance. You have a general idea where the treasure is. Perhaps I can locate it with magic before the beholder goes after it. At least we can try!"

Together you hurry off across the desolate terrain, wondering what dangers lie ahead and whether you'll ever survive long enough to complete your quest. . . .

THE END

"Don't be a fool," you think. "If you dive into the river and drown, then you'll be dead, Redbeard will probably die, and Jay will never know what became of you. But if you at least try to bargain with Scarface, you may be able to stay alive to help Redbeard and to see Jay again." You decide to bargain.

You grab your belt pouch and hold it up for the scar-faced man to see. "Come a step closer and I'll throw this into the river!" you shout.

"Do that and it's curtains for you!" snarls Scarface, but you notice that he and his men come to a halt.

"Look, if I give you the map, will you promise not to kill me or Redbeard?" you ask. You know his promise probably won't be worth anything, but once he has the map, he won't have any need to kill you.

"I don't care one bit whether you live or die," Scarface says, "but if you give me the map, I won't waste my time bothering to kill you."

You know that's as close to a promise as you'll ever get from Scarface. Keeping your fingers crossed for luck, you toss the pouch to him. He pulls it open and glances hurriedly at the map. "Come on," he says to his men, and they set off across the bridge at a run.

You breathe a sigh of relief, then hurry to Redbeard's side. He has struggled to sit up and holds one hand to his side. You see blood seeping between his fingers.

"Sorry I . . . let you down, Sparrow," he gasps.

You didn't, Redbeard," you insist. "I'm just glad you're alive! But I've got to get you to a doctor!"

"Sparrow! Sparrow!" you hear a voice call. You look up and see your brother Jay running across the bridge toward you.

"Jay!" you shout joyfully. Then you remember what has just happened. "I—I'm sorry, Jay. I don't have the map anymore. I had to give it up to save our lives."

"I know, Sparrow. I saw what happened," says Jay. "I was afraid they'd kill you. It's okay that you gave them the map. It doesn't matter, as long as you're alive."

Together you carry Redbeard across the bridge into Riverbend. You're sorry the spirit of Farad Silverhair won't be put to rest, and you're sorry you'll never be rich. But at least you and Jay are together again. And you've made a good friend—who now needs your help.

THE END

"I think you're right, Jay. We've got to go try to find the treasure by ourselves," you tell your brother. "Redbeard is badly wounded, and it may take him a long time to get well. We're going to need a lot of money to take care of him and keep us all fed and everything. We need that treasure to do it!"

With the last of your money, you buy two spears so that you'll be armed against whatever danger might be in the cave. With a branch and some oily rags, you make a torch to use inside the cave. You're as well prepared as you can be, so the next morning you set out, following the map through the hilly country outside town.

Toward afternoon, you find the hill marked on the map and follow an old, nearly invisible trail up its side. Near the rocky crest, you spot a dark opening in the hillside—the treasure cave!

With flint and steel, Jay lights the torch. He looks at you and gives a strained grin. "Good luck, Sparrow," he says.

"Good luck to you, too, Jay," you echo. Your heart is pounding and your legs are trembling. Jay leads the way into the cave cautiously, torch in one hand and spear in the other. You're right behind him, clutching your spear. Slowly the two of you move down a narrow, rocky passageway. You come to a corner and edge around it carefully.

In the torchlight, you see a large cavern. Someone, probably the bandits who hid the

treasure here, has stretched a net of thick ropes across the middle of the cavern. And on the other side of the net, in a corner, is a pile of chests and bags!

"There it is!" you exclaim excitedly.

Glancing hurriedly to both sides, the two of you move forward to push aside the net and get at the treasure. But as your arms and hands touch the rope, you discover that it is smeared with thick, sticky glue. You both pull and tug, but you only get stuck worse. Even your spears are stuck. In his efforts to get free, Jay drops the torch.

Suddenly, with a shock of terror, you realize what is happening—and what the dying man who gave you the map was trying to warn you of.

"Jay!" you shriek. "This isn't a net—it's a giant spiderweb!"

You both raise your eyes to peer upward through the gloom in agonized horror. The light from the torch flickering on the floor of the cave gleams upon six staring eyes of a huge, hairy spider, as big as a horse, which is slowly creeping down the web toward you.

THE END

"We really don't know much about Rogaldo, Jay," you think aloud. "He may have been planning with this other magician to cheat us all along! I say we should go get the treasure ourselves! If we find out Rogaldo's honest, we can always share with him later."

Late the next afternoon, you find the cave you are seeking high on a rocky hillside. Jay takes out his flint and steel and lights the torches you have brought with you. Suddenly there is a sharp crack, like a clap of thunder, and Rogaldo appears before you!

"So," he says, frowning, "you choose to betray me despite my help! Very well! I'll see that the king's bones are buried, and I'll take only whatever magical tools I may find—but I put upon you the spell of forgetfulness. For five years, you will remember nothing of the treasure or the meaning of the map you carry!" And with that, Rogaldo vanishes.

As if awakening from a trance, you blink and look around. "What are we doing here, anyway, Jay?" you ask, puzzled.

"I—I seem to recall looking for something, but I can't remember what." He looks worried. "Something strange is going on, Sparrow!"

"It's getting late. We'd better get back to town, Jay. Once we're there, maybe we can figure out what's going on."

Puzzled, worried, and strangely sad, you start back on the road toward Riverbend.

THE END

Frozen with fear, you crouch beside Redbeard, waiting to see what the giant dinosaur will do. Suddenly it sees you, and it pauses, as if it is looking you over. Then it simply crashes on by through the swamp.

Redbeard heaves a sigh of relief. "We were in luck," he says. "It's a plant-eater."

You start off again, trudging over the soggy path. From time to time, will-o-the-wisps drift alongside you, then suddenly vanish to reappear in a different place to confuse you and try to make you leave the path. But Redbeard plods steadily on, and you follow him, ignoring the eerie floating lights. Weird noises fill the night. Once, a huge batlike shape skims across the face of the moon, and another time you see a huge glowing shape moving in the distance.

But as the first faint light of dawn creeps into the sky, you begin to notice that the ground is becoming firmer. Patches of grass occasionally appear among the bulrushes and cattails. Before long you are out of the marsh.

"We're safe now," Redbeard says thankfully. His mouth stretches in a huge yawn. "We need some sleep, Sparrow. Let's rest awhile before we move on." You eagerly agree, and the two of you drop onto the soft grass and are soon sound asleep.

You can tell by the sun that it's nearly noon when you awaken. You share a quick meal of bread and cheese, then start out once more. Soon you come to the road, and before long you see the wooden bridge that crosses the river into the town of Riverbend, where you hope your brother Jay will be waiting.

But when you reach the bridge, half a dozen figures suddenly spring out of hiding from a thick cluster of bushes nearby. Your heart leaps to your throat as you recognize Scarface and his crew! Before Redbeard can even draw his sword, one of the orcs stabs him and he falls to the ground. Scarface stalks grimly toward you, sword in hand!

Two ideas flash into your mind. You could try to bargain with Scarface, offering him the map if he'll spare your life. If he agrees, you'll survive and you'll be able to help the injured Redbeard—but it will mean the end of your quest. Your other idea is to dive into the river and try to escape. But you don't know how deep or how swift the river is, so you'll be risking your life—and you'll be deserting Redbeard. You have only seconds to make up your mind. What should you do?

1) If you decide to use the map to bargain with Scarface, turn to page 109.

2) If you decide to dive in the river and try to escape, turn to page 56.

The left bank seems a bit closer, so you strike out frantically in that direction. In a few moments, you are pulling yourself up over the roots of a twisted, gnarled mangrove tree onto muddy ground. There is no sign of the monster now.

"Jay, where are you?" you call frantically.

"Over here, Sparrow!" You follow Jay's voice through the bulrushes. Soaked to the skin, you crouch beside one another.

"We're in real danger, Sparrow. We've got to get out of here," says Jay. "Come on!"

Following the river, you plod through bulrushes and cattails. Fortunately, dawn comes soon, and with it, the noises of the marsh die out. By midmorning, you are finally out of the marsh.

"Thank goodness!" you exclaim. You put your hand to your belt to give it a hitch, then stop dead. The pouch that hung from your belt, the pouch in which you carried the map, is gone! "Jay! I lost the pouch in the marsh!"

"Not the pouch with the map in it!"

You feel as if you're going to burst into tears, but then you straighten up and take a deep breath. "Maybe it won't matter, Jay. We know the treasure is in the hills outside Riverbend. We'll search every chance we get. Come on!"

You march determinedly toward Riverbend, your only hope that you'll find the treasure and the bones of Farad Silverhair—someday.

THE END

"Maybe if we hurry we can get through the desert without meeting any of the really dangerous creatures," you suggest.

"That's logical," agrees Rogaldo. "The desert road it is, then."

The patches of grass beside the road become fewer and fewer, and soon you are walking through a bleak, parched desert dotted with scrubby bushes. All day long you watch fearfully for sight of one of the dangerous creatures Rogaldo said live in this place, but you don't see anything except a few small lizards.

When night comes, you build a fire and Rogaldo puts a magic barrier around the campsite. "It will keep out poisonous snakes and other such small things, but some of the bigger creatures would be able to get through it," he explains.

You have a little trouble falling asleep after what Rogaldo said. However, there are no problems during the night, and in the morning you set out once more. "We should be out of the desert and onto the road to Riverbend by early afternoon," Rogaldo predicts.

But only moments later, he suddenly halts and peers at the sky, shading his eyes with his hand. Far ahead, high in the sky, you see a tiny speck. As you watch, it grows larger and larger. It's heading straight toward you!

"It's a brass dragon!" exclaims Rogaldo.

"Is it dangerous?" Jay asks anxiously.

"That depends," says the wizard. "Sometimes brass dragons merely want to talk.

Then they're completely harmless. But if this one is coming to attack us, we're in serious danger!"

"Can you fight it with magic?" you ask.

"Only if I attack first. If I can catch it by surprise with a blast of magical energy, I might be able to destroy it. We have to decide what to do. If we wait to see if it wants to talk and it attacks instead, we're doomed. But attacking it could be a big mistake."

You can see the dragon clearly now as if flies swiftly toward you. It is at least thirty feet long, with great batlike wings.

"What shall we do?" asks Rogaldo. "Wait to see if it only wants to talk, or try to blast it first?"

1) If you decide you must attack the dragon before it attacks you, turn to page 41.

2) If you decide to wait and see if the dragon wants to talk, turn to page 66.

You can't bring yourself to go look for the treasure without your brother Jay. After all, it's his quest, too!

You spend the whole next day waiting at the bridge that leads into Riverbend. You feel sure that's where Jay will come into the town. Many people come up the road and cross the bridge, but Jay isn't one of them. He still hasn't shown up by the end of the day.

That night, as you and Redbeard are sitting at an inn having supper, a black-cloaked figure enters the inn and looks around. When he sees you, he starts to stalk toward your table. You gasp as you see that it's Scarface! With an oath, Redbeard reaches for his sword.

"Keep your sword sheathed, warrior. I've come to talk, not to fight," growls Scarface. "I have a feeling this lad is waiting for his brother. Well, he's not going to show up, because we have him! If you want him, give me the map and I'll release him to you. Otherwise I'll cut his throat!"

"I—I've got to give him the map, Redbeard!" you tell your friend. "I have no choice!"

He nods slowly. "Of course you must, lad."

"I'll take the map now," demands Scarface. You take it out of your pouch and hand it to him. Scarface grins evilly. "We have your brother right outside. I'll bring him in." He hurries from the room. Moments later, he returns with two of his gang and your brother. Then he and his men hurry from the room.

"Jay!" you exclaim. "Are you all right?"

"They haven't been feeding me very well, but otherwise I'm okay. They were waiting at the bridge and grabbed me before I saw them."

You introduce Jay and Redbeard, then quickly tell Jay about your adventures.

Jay sighs. "I'm sorry you had to give up the map for me after all the troubles you've had, Sparrow. I'm afraid poor King Farad's bones will never be buried now—and you and I will be poor all our lives."

Redbeard leans forward and says, "You know, we don't have to give up yet! Scarface and his gang will have to wait for sunrise before they can start out after the treasure. We can get ourselves some horses tonight, camp outside of town, and follow them. We'll let him lead us to the cave and then—well, we'll just see what happens. It will be dangerous, of course. Well? Do you want to try my plan?"

1) If you decide to follow Scarface and his men, turn to page 82.

2) If you decide it would be too dangerous to follow Scarface, turn to page 144.

It's not an easy choice, but it seems to you that it might be easier to deal with monsters than with ghosts, wights, or any of the other sorts of things that might be found in a haunted place. After all, those things were all DEAD, and how can you fight something that's already dead? But you feel you can trust Redbeard and his sword to deal with most any live monster you might encounter.

"Let's head through the Marsh of Monsters," you announce in a voice that sounds braver than you feel.

As soon as it gets dark enough, you and Redbeard sneak away from the campfire, leaving the road behind. For a long time you trudge side by side through the moonlight. Then you become aware that the ground underfoot is turning soft and damp, and the meadow grass is giving way to tall cattails and other wetlands vegetation. You realize with a shiver that you must be entering the Marsh of Monsters!

"Stay close beside me," Redbeard urges. "There are some deep pools, plus quicksand all about. Stay on this narrow path."

You should be sleepy at this time of night, but fear and excitement keep you wide awake. You clutch the hem of Redbeard's leather tunic so that you won't stray away from him.

Suddenly you notice three round glowing lights off to one side of the path, seeming to float along beside you. Then you see two more on the other side.

"What—what are those lights?" you wonder aloud.

"Will-o-the-wisps," answers Redbeard. "Foul creatures that feed upon death! They'll try to lead us into deep water or quicksand. Don't watch them."

The marsh is noisy with the buzz and whir of insects, but there are many unknown noises, too. Off in the distance you hear a loud bellowing, and in another direction something is making a weird wailing sound. Nearby you hear a loud rustling as some large creature thrashes through the thick forest of tall cattails.

With a twinge of terror, you realize that the sound is coming straight toward you and Redbeard! Moments later, a huge shape looms up no more than fifty paces away. Moonlight shimmers on its giant scaly body, and its eyes glow with a pale green light. It's a dinosaur!

You know that some dinosaurs are harmless, but if this one is a flesh-eater, you and Redbeard are doomed! If you run, you may have a chance of escaping before it sees you—but you'll also run the risk of falling into quicksand, getting lost forever in the swamp, or even running straight into some other deadly monster. What should you do?

1) If you decide to run, turn to page 76.

2) If you decide to stay and see if the dinosaur is harmless, turn to page 115.

The tower looks dark and forbidding. "Let's keep going, Jay!" you say.

Before long, you can see that there are indeed lights ahead. In about an hour, you reach the town and find a fair going on—an excellent chance to make some money! Quickly you go to where the crowd is thickest and begin your juggling act. Soon you're surrounded by applauding people. When your act is over, you both pass among the crowd and collect four large fistfuls of coins!

You and Jay divide the money, then decide to split up, agreeing to meet later.

When you meet again, Jay acts excited. "There's a bridge here," he announces. "We can leave tomorrow morning." Then his eyes widen. "Sparrow! Where is your pouch?"

You glance down and see that your belt pouch, which contained all your money and the map, is gone! The two strings that fastened it to your belt have been cut. You know at once what has happened—a pickpocket in the crowd has cut your pouch strings with sharp scissors. You've been robbed!

"It's all right, Sparrow," Jay says bravely. "We know the cave is somewhere in the hills beyond Riverbend. We'll still find the treasure and bury the king's bones!"

You nod, but there's a lump in your throat. You know that, without the map, there's little chance you'll ever be able to find the cave.

THE END

You decide to head for the bridge. That's probably where Jay will be waiting if he's reached Riverbend. You hope Scarface and his gang have given up looking for you by now.

The sun is low and red by the time you arrive at the wooden bridge that crosses the river into Riverbend. Suddenly half a dozen figures leap out from among the bushes growing beside the bridge. Scarface and his crew!

"Kill 'em!" snarls Scarface.

"Do your best, Sparrow!" yells Redbeard.

Quickly you yank out the sword from the wight's den. Scarface and three of his band attack Redbeard, and two more come after you. You know you haven't a chance, but you decide to go down fighting. Gritting your teeth, you aim a blow at your nearest attacker.

To your amazement, the sword feels as light as a twig. It hisses through the air and slices into the man's hand. Howling, he drops his sword and clutches his bleeding fingers.

The second man thrusts his sword at you, but the point simply bounces off the chain mail shirt you took from the wight's den. As you lunge at him, he backs away quickly—and falls off the bridge into the river!

Astounded, you turn to see if you can help Redbeard. Two of his opponents are down, and the other two are desperately trying to avoid his flashing sword, which is glowing and making a loud humming sound. Looking down at your sword, you see the same thing!

"Magic!" exclaims Scarface. "We haven't

got a chance!" He turns and runs, his band following after him. Redbeard stares hard at his sword and fingers his coat of mail.

"These swords and coats of armor are magic, Sparrow!" he exclaims. "Lucky for us that we stopped to explore that wight's den!"

"Sparrow! Sparrow!" you hear a voice call, and you look up to see Jay running across the bridge toward you. You run to meet him and pound him on the back joyfully.

That night, with a coin from the wight's treasure, the three of you have a feast at an inn. You tell Jay about all your adventures.

He stares at you, shaking his head. "You could have been killed, Sparrow! I think we ought to forget this quest!"

You stare at him, shocked. "But, Jay—we promised to put the king's spirit to rest! And what about the treasure?"

"You've already got plenty of gold from the wight's den," says Jay. "Look—why not give the map to Redbeard and let him complete the quest?" He puts a hand on your shoulder. "I promised our mother on her deathbed to look after you. I don't want you risking your life any more. If you decide to finish the quest, I'll go with you—but I wish you'd do as I ask!"

1) If you decide to let Redbeard continue the quest alone, turn to page 15.

2) But if you decide to continue on with the quest, turn to page 68.

"Well, we won't meet up with any more giant frogs on the ROAD, but we may if we stay near the river," you declare. "Let's head for the road, Jay."

But you haven't gone fifty steps before you realize that you are entering a huge marsh. The ground is soft and squishy underfoot, and a forest of high bulrushes and cattails surrounds the two of you.

The noises coming from all parts of the marsh hint of strange creatures inhabiting it. In the distance, you hear a loud bellow that must come from the throat of some enormous monster. Much nearer, you hear a long, wailing shriek. Nearer still, there is a low, steady grunting noise.

You stop suddenly. "Jay, I don't think we'd better try to get through here after all," you decide. "It's too dangerous. There are all sorts of strange things in this marsh, and some of them could be a lot worse than those giant frogs! I wouldn't be surprised if there's quicksand, too. I don't think we could possibly make it all the way to the road."

Jay nods as he looks around. "I'm afraid you're right, Sparrow. We'd better turn back and keep following the riverbank after all."

Please turn to page 13.

You can't just leave the frightened little cub, perhaps to die. You've got to help it!

The cub bares its teeth as you approach. You begin tugging on the branches until finally it scrambles free. It shakes itself, eyes you for a moment, then scurries off.

You sigh, wishing you knew your way as well as the bear does. You trudge along, hoping you'll somehow be able to find your way out of the forest. But as time goes on, you realize you could wander through these woods until you die of thirst and hunger. Finally you sink to the ground, weary and frightened.

Suddenly you sense you're not alone. You look up and see the figure of a huge bear towering over you! So quickly that you mistrust your eyes, the bear changes into a huge, burly, shaggy man. You realize you are facing one of the most dreaded of all creatures—a werebear!

"Fear not," the figure says in a deep voice. "You helped my little one, and I wish to repay you. Follow me."

You follow the figure through the trees. Suddenly you notice dark, four-footed shapes all around you. A wolf pack!

"You need not fear them," the werebear says calmly. "They dare not attack with me here."

Within a short time, you are out of the woods and back on the road. A short distance down the road, you see a building with a sign swinging in the breeze. It must be the inn your brother told you about! You turn to thank your rescuer, but the werebear has vanished.

You hurry toward the inn, hoping to find Jay there. But when you arrive, the inn is empty except for the innkeeper and a brawny, red-bearded warrior with a sword at his hip.

"Please, sir," you say to the innkeeper, "I'm a juggler. May I perform for your guests tonight for some coins to buy supper?"

"I'll buy your supper if you're any good, lad," booms the red beard. Grinning, you take out your colored wooden balls and start your act. Redbeard applauds appreciatively.

Suddenly the door bursts open. You look up to see the scar-faced man and two of his band!

"It's one of those kids!" snarls Scarface as his eyes light on you. "Seize him!"

The other two move toward you, but suddenly the red-bearded warrior thrusts himself in front of them, sword drawn. "Hold!" he growls. "What do you want with this lad?"

"Kill this lout!" Scarface orders. The air is filled with the ring of blade on blade as the innkeeper flees in terror.

In the confusion, the door has been left unguarded. You could run to safety—but the red-bearded warrior has risked his life to help you. Should you stay and try to help him, or should you escape before it's too late?

1) If you decide to escape while you can, turn to page 12.

2) If you decide to stay and help the red-bearded warrior, turn to page 100.

"If there's no way to tell for sure, why don't we just flip a coin?" you suggest.

"Why not indeed?" Rogaldo shrugs and pulls a coin from his belt pouch. "Heads we go north, tails we go south." He flips the coin into the air, catches it, and slaps it on his wrist. "Heads. North it is!"

Daybreak is still hours away, but Rogaldo rouses the stable owner and buys three fast horses. Soon your steeds are trotting swiftly up the north road out of Riverbend.

"He can't be more than a day ahead of us," Rogaldo says grimly. "We'll catch him!"

You move at a steady pace all morning. Near noon, you stop briefly to let the horses rest and browse and to eat lunch yourselves. Then you press on all afternoon and into the evening, stopping only when it is too dark to travel safely. As soon as it is light, you're off again.

The second day goes by almost exactly as the first. Late in the afternoon on the third day, Rogaldo leans forward on his mount and points. "There he is!" Far in the distance, you see several tiny, indistinct shapes.

You urge your horses to a gallop. As you draw closer, the shapes become distinct—a robed figure on horseback leading four other heavily laden horses. It must be the treasure!

They don't seem to be moving very fast, perhaps because of the heavy loads they carry, and you quickly close the distance. The figure in the lead doesn't even seem to notice that you're behind him.

You follow as Rogaldo urges his horse forward until he is alongside one of the four packhorses. He leans out and stretches a hand toward the horse.

The moment Rogaldo touches it, the horses and the man all vanish into thin air!

Rogaldo reigns his horse to a stop, and you and Jay pull up alongside him. "We've been following the illusion instead of the real Vuverain," he says bitterly.

"Can't you locate the real Vuverain with the crystal ball?" you plead, hoping against hope.

Rogaldo shakes his head. "He's far out of range now. There's no chance."

You hang your head, fighting back tears. The quest is ended. You've failed.

Rogaldo sighs. "Well, I guess there's nothing for me to do but head back to my tower. What about you two?"

"We may as well go back to Riverbend," Jay says slowly. "Sparrow and I can probably find work entertaining at an inn."

"I'll know where to find you if need be, then. I intend to continue trying to locate Vuverain. And if I ever find out where he is, I'll get in touch with you and we'll pay him a visit." Rogaldo grins wickedly and winks.

You and Jay exchange hopeful glances. With the wizard's help, perhaps some day soon the quest will be fulfilled after all!

THE END

You know that small frogs frighten easily. Maybe big ones do, too. Taking a deep breath, you begin to yell and wave your arms wildly.

The air is suddenly filled with frightened frogs, leaping off in every direction.

"It worked!" you sigh. "We'd better stay awake to make sure they don't come back."

The river flows through a marshy area, and soon a forest of bulrushes and cattails, full of night sounds, stretches away on all sides. In the distance, you hear loud bellowing. Nearby, a huge creature crashes through the bulrushes. You and Jay crouch in silence, hoping you don't run into any more trouble.

Trouble does come, however, so swiftly that you are stunned. A huge pair of jaws, ringed with spikelike teeth, suddenly erupts out of the water and bites into your raft, splitting it in two. You and Jay are flung into the water.

You come up gasping, aware that you had better get out of the river FAST before those huge, toothy jaws chomp on YOU! You have no idea where Jay is or which way he's swimming, and you don't want to wind up on opposite sides of the river. Both banks of the river seem fairly close—but should you swim for the left bank or the right?

1) If you decide to swim to the left bank, turn to page 117.

2) If you decide to swim to the right bank, turn to page 105.

You scratch your head as you try to decide
what to do. You really feel you ought to wait
for Jay, but you have to face the fact that he
might not show up for days. Now that you're
so close to the treasure, wouldn't it be smarter
to make sure of getting it once and for all?
Besides, while you're waiting, someone else
might accidentally find the treasure!

"I think we'd better go get the treasure right
away, Redbeard," you decide. You hope Jay
won't be angry that you didn't wait for him,
once you explain your reasons.

You and Redbeard together have just
enough money to take a room for the night at
an inn, to buy a spear for you so that you'll be
able to help him fight whatever danger you
might find in the cave, and to get a few provisions for the journey into the hills—a loaf of
bread and a large round of soft cheese.

In the morning, you start out, following the
map through the hilly country beyond Riverbend. It's midafternoon before you find the hill
on which, according to the map, the treasure
cave is located. You start up the hillside, following the faint trail indicated on the map.
You're better than halfway to the top when
Redbeard suddenly stops and peers down at a
patch of ground alongside the trail. "Look
here, Sparrow," he says excitedly.

The patch of ground is muddy from a recent
rainstorm, and in the mud there is a clear
print of a huge, bare human foot!

"That's a giant's footprint or I'm a goblin,"

mutters Redbeard. "It's no more than a day or two old. If there's a giant living on this hill, it may well make its home in the treasure cave, Sparrow. That must be the danger the man who gave you the map was trying to warn you of!"

"What kind of giant do you suppose it is?" you ask anxiously. You know there are several different kinds of giants, and while some are harmless—even helpful—to humans, others can be extremely dangerous.

"In this place, probably a hill giant," says Redbeard, "or possibly a stone giant. But whatever kind it is, you can bet it's guarding the treasure, Sparrow, and we'll have to fight it!"

Redbeard shakes his head and looks worried. You're worried, too—can the two of you overcome a huge, muscular giant?

"Well, shall we keep going?" asks Redbeard. "I'm willing if you are."

You simply can't give up without at least finding out a little more. Maybe the giant doesn't live in the cave after all. Maybe it's not even anywhere on the hill now. "Let's keep going," you say.

You continue on up the trail, moving much more cautiously and quietly now. Near the top, you edge around a large boulder and see the cave about a hundred paces farther up the trail. You also see the giant, who is sitting beside the cave entrance, dozing in the sunshine. It is a huge, red-skinned, black-haired

hill giant. Beside it lies a club the size of a small tree!

"We could try to rush the giant," whispers Redbeard. "We might have a chance if we could reach it before it wakes up."

Something you see on the rocky hillside gives you an idea. "Redbeard, hill giants aren't very smart, are they?" you ask in a whisper.

Redbeard nods his head from side to side. "Hill giants aren't much brighter than a four- or five-year-old child. Why?"

"Well, maybe we can trick it," you suggest and proceed to explain your idea.

Redbeard listens anxiously. "You'd be taking a terrible risk," he whispers when you finish, "but it's your decision, Sparrow!"

1) If you decide to try Redbeard's plan to attack the giant, turn to page 104.

2) If you decide instead to try your plan to trick the giant, turn to page 147.

You feel that Jay is probably right—the raft wouldn't be safe. You glance up and down the riverbank. "Which way shall we go?" you ask Jay.

"When you're not sure, right is right," Jay suggests, as you've heard him say many times before in similar situations. So you turn to the right and begin walking along the riverbank.

You haven't gone far when a loud snort and a splash from the river startle you. Some huge creature has come up to the surface for a moment, and you catch a glimpse of a huge scaly body, with yellow eyes and a gaping mouth full of sharp teeth. It's a good thing you decided not to ride the raft down the river!

After you've trudged along for a while, Jay pauses for a moment, peering through the gathering darkness. "I think I see some sort of building ahead," he says. "Where there's a building by a river, there could be a bridge."

You hurry on, and before long you reach the building. It is a windowless round tower, about three floors high and made of rough, dark stone. A short flight of stone steps leads up to a single closed door.

There is no sign of a bridge over the river here, as you and Jay had hoped. "Maybe we ought to ask whoever lives here if we're heading the right way," you suggest.

Jay studies the tower, chewing his lip thoughtfully. "I don't know, Sparrow. I don't like the looks of this place. Who would want to live alone out here in such a dark, gloomy-looking building?" He peers off into the distance. "I think I see lights way over there. Maybe it's a town. If there's a town by the river, there must be a bridge. I think we ought to keep going and see."

It's nearly dark now, and you remember how the goblins caught you because you were out in the open at night. You think about the huge creature you saw in the river—maybe it comes up onto the land at night to hunt! It might not be a good idea to keep going through the darkness. Maybe whoever lives in the tower will let you spend the night safe inside. Should you knock on the door and ask?

1) If you decide to keep on going toward the lights in the distance, turn to page 126.

2) If you decide to knock on the tower door, turn to page 44.

You think you'd be safer on land than floating on the water on a flimsy raft while you
sleep, so you decide to stay where you are.
There's a bit of a chill in the air, so you build
up the fire and lie down, one on each side of it.
Before long you're asleep.

Suddenly you're awakened by a crushing
weight on your chest! Your eyes fly open, and
with astonishment you see a small burly,
black-bearded man kneeling on you, holding a
knife at your throat! It's a robber dwarf! Out
of the corner of your eye, you see two other
dwarfs holding Jay down.

"Don't move or I'll cut your throat!" the
dwarf growls. With his free hand, he pulls the
pouch off your belt. Then he picks up your food
bag from where you placed it by the fire, and
in an instant he and the other two robbers
have vanished into the night.

"Sparrow! Are you all right?" calls Jay.

You sit up. "Yes, but they've taken my pouch
with the map in it!"

Jay puts his arm around your shoulder and
tries to comfort you. "Well, there's nothing we
can do about it. It looks like the end of our
quest, but we can still ride the raft to Riverbend. We'll find work there, at an inn or some-
place. We'll get along all right. You'll see,
Sparrow!"

THE END

You look from Redbeard to your brother and back to Redbeard again. "I'm sorry," you say, "but I just don't want to risk my life, or yours either, anymore! I'd have been eaten by wolves if I hadn't been saved by a werebear, and then Redbeard saved me from Scarface, and we were attacked by a wight and a carrion crawler, and then a nixie tried to make us slaves. I've faced enough danger! I'm satisfied with the the treasure I got from the wight's lair. There's enough to buy us food and lodging for a long time, Jay!"

"But what about the spirit of poor King Farad Silverhair?" he asks softly. You put your head down and don't answer.

Redbeard looks at you for a long time. "I didn't think this would be your answer, Sparrow," he says. He gets up and slowly walks out the door and into the street. You have a terrible feeling that you'll never see him again!

You've lost a good friend, and it looks as if you've lost a lot of your brother's respect. You feel guilty about not trying harder to help free the spirit of Farad Silverhair. You're beginning to fear that you may regret this decision for the rest of your life.

THE END

You decide you can't risk offending these warriors who have saved you, and you agree to go meet their king. You and Jay each climb up behind a rider, and soon you're galloping over the plain.

After a long ride, you come to a large town standing at the foot of a hill. High on the hill stands an imposing castle. You are taken up to the castle and into a cheerful, sunlit kitchen, where you are given a fine meal of cold roast chicken, fresh bread, and greens.

That evening, you do your juggling act for the elderly king and his courtiers after their dinner. The king smiles at your tricks and applauds loudly when you finish your performance. Then he beckons you toward him.

"You are fine jugglers," he says, sounding very pleased. "Would you believe that there isn't another juggler in my whole land? How would you like to stay here and serve as my Royal Jugglers?"

The offer would have seemed too good to be true a day ago, but now you are committed to completing your quest.

"Your Majesty, you do us great honor, and we thank you from the bottom of our hearts," says Jay. "But we are on a quest, and we have promised to—"

"I do not care to be refused when I offer an act of kindness!" the king interrupts. "Guards! Let these two cool off in a dungeon until they learn some manners!"

Before you know it, you and Jay are being

hauled away by burly guards and pushed into a damp, dark room deep in the bowels of the castle. "When you agree to accept the king's request, knock three times," says one guard as he slams the cell door shut.

"I was afraid something like this would happen," Jay groans. "Well, it looks like we'll have to agree to become the king's jugglers, Sparrow. But the first chance we get, we'll escape and finish the quest!"

You nod sadly. You are afraid that the king is going to have you so closely watched that you'll never be able to escape. Someday you still may be able to keep your promise to bury King Farad Silverhair and gain the treasure, but you know that day is now far, far in the future. . . .

THE END

"I don't think trying to trick the giant is any riskier than attacking it," you argue with Redbeard. "And if it works, we'll get King Farad's bones and at least half the treasure without having to fight!"

"All right, Sparrow," Redbeard agrees reluctantly. "May luck be with you. If you do run into trouble, I'll help as best as I can."

Opening up your bag of provisions, you remove the round of cheese and carefully slip it under your jacket, grateful that you and Redbeard didn't stop for lunch because your whole idea depends on this cheese! With your heart pounding, you step out from behind the boulder and saunter toward the slumbering giant, whistling, trying hard to appear braver than you feel.

Immediately the giant awakens with a start. Snarling, it reaches for its club. Then, as you continue to approach with no sign of fear, it looks puzzled. So far your plan is working just as you hoped. Seeing an unarmed boy, the giant doesn't know what to make of things.

"Me Gorgo! Who YOU? What you do here?" it finally bellows in a deep voice.

"Why, I'm Sparrow, and I've come to share the treasure in the cave with you, Mr. Gorgo," you announce with a smile.

Now the giant is really puzzled. It frowns and scratches its head thoughtfully. "But treasure MINE!" it roars. "Why should Gorgo share treasure with YOU?"

You smile pleasantly and say, "Well, you see,

Mr. Gorgo, I am the strongest man in the world, much stronger than you are. If we were to fight, you would surely get hurt. But if we share the treasure, we won't have to fight and I won't have to hurt you."

The giant frowns as it thinks that over for a long time. At last it roars, "YOU stronger than GORGO?"

"Yes indeed," you tell him. "Allow me to show you." You turn around and walk over to a pile of rocks nearby. Squatting down with your back toward the giant, you carefully slide the cheese out from under your jacket. The pale tan lump of soft cheese is almost exactly the same color and shape as the rocks. When you stand up and turn around holding the cheese, it looks as if you've picked up one of the rocks.

"Watch carefully," you tell the giant. "I will now squeeze water out of this rock!" You begin squeezing the soft cheese with both hands. The watery whey gushes out of it and splashes to the ground. You continue to squeeze until the cheese is pressed flat, then toss it into a nearby clump of bushes.

You bend down, pick up a real rock from the pile, and toss it to the giant. "Now you try it. Then we'll know who is stronger."

Gorgo looks at the rock, then puts it between its huge hands and squeezes. The giant grits its teeth, and the veins on its neck stand out and its red skin begins to turn purple. At last Gorgo stops squeezing and looks at the

unchanged rock. "Gorgo can't!" it pants, puzzled.

"Of course not," you say quickly. "And that's why we shouldn't fight—because I'm so much stronger than you that I'd hurt you. So if we share the treasure, we can be friends and we won't have to fight. Okay?"

The giant looks confused, then glances once more at the rock in its hands and shakes its head. "Okay," it says finally.

"Good," you say. "Then you go into the cave and bring out the treasure, and I'll take my half and leave."

You breathe a sigh as the giant turns and lumbers into the cave. It returns again and again until there is a large pile of bags and chests piled on the ground in front of you.

"I'm going to call my servant to carry my share," you explain to the giant. "Don't pay any attention to him. He's not strong like I am." You turn your head and call, "Redbeard!"

Redbeard has heard everything and comes running to your side. You notice that he has removed his sword, so as not to rouse the giant's suspicion. "Yes, master? What is your command?" he asks meekly.

"Pick up our share of the treasure and carry it," you say with a lordly air. You spot the bag that contains King Farad's bones and pick it up, along with a small bag of coins. Redbeard picks up as much as he can carry.

"Gorgo, we are now friends forever," you say

to the huge creature. "If you ever need my great strength for anything, let me know and I will come and help you."

"That good. Gorgo thank you," it says slowly, obviously trying to figure out what has happened. You decide you had better leave quickly.

"Let's get out of here fast, Redbeard!" you whisper to the warrior. Resisting the desire to run, you trudge quickly down the path past the boulder. Once you are out of the giant's sight, you do break into a run until you reach the bottom of the hill.

"Sparrow, you did it!" chuckles Redbeard. "You flummoxed that poor giant until it didn't even know which way was up! You've fulfilled the quest good and proper, I'd say—we have Farad's bones and enough treasure to make us all rich for life."

"I sure hope Jay has reached Riverbend by the time we get back," you say with a grin. "What a story I have to tell him!"

THE END

You really want to wait for Jay, but it could be several days before he shows up. Since you're this close to the treasure, it seems foolish not to get it at once—after all, what if, while you were waiting for Jay, someone chanced to discover the treasure and took it?

On horses you purchase with some of the wight's gold, you and Redbeard set out early the next morning. The map leads you among the hills beyond Riverbend and finally takes you up a rocky slope, where you find the entrance to a cave.

"This must be where the king's bones and the treasure are hidden!" says Redbeard, lighting a pair of torches.

"We've got to be careful," you say. "The man who gave Jay and me the map tried to warn us of something."

You enter the cave, each with a torch in one hand and a magical sword in the other. You move cautiously through a narrow, winding passageway. Rounding a corner, you find that the passageway suddenly widens into a large chamber. Someone—probably the robbers—has hung a huge net of thick ropes from the cave's ceiling. On the other side of the net, you spot a cluster of chests and bulging bags in the torchlight.

"The treasure!" you exclaim. Forgetting to be careful, you rush forward to push the net aside with your arm. But suddenly you find that you are stuck—the lengths of rope are covered with a thick gluelike substance!

"Look out, Sparrow!" yells Redbeard, darting to your side. Your eyes follow his wide-eyed gaze to the cave ceiling. With a shock of horror, you realize this isn't a net you're stuck to—it's a giant spiderweb! And there, crouched at the top of the web, its six eyes gleaming at you in the torchlight, is a huge hairy spider!

Your sword and Redbeard's begin to glow and hum. Redbeard lifts his blade toward the spider, and the creature immediately cowers back against the rocky ceiling.

"It's afraid of the sword's magic!" says Redbeard. "See if you can hack yourself loose while I hold the creature at bay."

You drop your torch and take your sword in your free left hand. To your relief, the magic sword easily cuts through the thick rope. When you are free, you hack a hole in the web and crawl through. Hurriedly you begin to tug chests and bags through the hole.

Minutes later, the treasure is piled outside the cave. With shovels you brought along, you and Redbeard dig a grave for the bones of King Farad Silverhair. You lower the bag of bones into the grave, then carefully cover the hole so that no one could ever find it. "Sleep well, great king," you murmur.

Then you and Redbeard load the treasure on the horses and head back toward Riverbend. You hope you'll find Jay there, but if you don't, you're confident you'll find him somehow.

THE END

It seems to you that it ought to be up to Rogaldo whether or not he wants to take on Vuverain in a duel to the death!

"I'm willing to do whatever you decide," you tell the wizard. "I'd gladly settle for King Silverhair's bones and half the treasure, but if you want to fight Vuverain, we'll stick by you—won't we, Jay?"

"Absolutely!" Jay says emphatically.

"Thanks for the vote of confidence, lads," Rogaldo says sincerely. "There's a lot at stake for you, too—I don't think for one moment he'd let you get away alive. But I believe I can beat this villain, and I owe him something!"

Rogaldo turns toward Vuverain and shouts fiercely, "I accept your challenge to a duel!"

Vuverain dismounts slowly and walks toward you. Rogaldo also dismounts and advances until he is about twenty paces from Vuverain. "You tell us when to start, Sparrow," Rogaldo calls out. "I'm ready!"

"I'm ready!" Vuverain echoes.

You pause for a moment, then shout, "Go!"

Instantly Vuverain vanishes, and in his place you see a forty-foot blue dragon! Your heart sinks as you realize the cunning of his choice. Besides being huge, blue dragons can shoot powerful bolts of lightning from their eyes. Rogaldo had better think fast or he's a goner! But what living thing can withstand a bolt of lightning?

Suddenly Rogaldo's form transforms itself into a jellylike black shape. For a moment, you think he's made a terrible mistake. Then you realize he has become a black pudding, which is invulnerable to lightning. And if the dragon tries to slash it to pieces, the pieces will just flow together and become one again. On the attack, black puddings ooze a liquid that can dissolve wood, even metal—and certainly the scaly skin of a dragon. The dragon seems to sense the danger as the black pudding crawls menacingly toward it.

"You've got him now, Rogaldo!" you yell excitedly.

Suddenly there is a loud POOF! and the blue dragon begins to change color. As you watch its scales turn from blue to purple to deep red, you gasp—red dragons breathe fire, and fire can destroy a black pudding!

"Change, Rogaldo!" Jay yells frantically. With a shimmer, the black pudding suddenly assumes the form of a ten-foot tower of stone. You realize it's a stone golem—a manlike creature made of stone. Its rock-hard exterior is oblivious to fire, but the golem's powerful stone fists can batter the dragon to a pulp.

As the golem begins to advance, the red dragon vanishes, and in its place you see a bulky grayish-yellow creature with huge, powerful claws—an umber hulk!

But before the umber hulk's crushing claws close on it, the golem transforms itself into a huge creature shaped like a giant centipede. It's a remorhaz, capable of swallowing the umber hulk in one gulp and burning it to

a crisp inside a body as hot as molten steel!

As the Remorhaz slithers forward, the hulk instantly changes into a small creature like a scaly rooster with a long, snakelike tail. For a brief moment, you feel Vuverain has surely made a fatal mistake, but then you realize with a shock that he has become a cockatrice! If the remorhaz so much as touches it, the remorhaz will be turned instantly to stone!

You gasp as the cockatrice darts forward. What can Rogaldo possibly change into now? A stone golem would be perfect, but he's already used that form.

The remorhaz stops suddenly, then, before your startled eyes, seems to melt into a slimy green puddle. You take heart as you realize that Rogaldo has become a green slime, a plantlike creature that feeds by dissolving the flesh of animals. The cockatrice can't stop itself and hurtles into the oozy green puddle. With a shriek of terror, the cockatrice begins to dissolve. In a few short minutes, it is gone.

Relief floods through you as the true Rogaldo appears once more. "Well, your quest is finally completed," he says. "You can bury King Silverhair's bones as you promised, you have enough treasure to make you rich as kings, and I have gained all of Vuverain's magic tools by defeating him. I'd say everyone should be happy"—he grins again—"except, of course, Vuverain!"

THE END

ENDLESS QUEST® Books
From the producers of the
DUNGEONS & DRAGONS® Game

- #1   DUNGEON OF DREAD
- #2   MOUNTAIN OF MIRRORS
- #3   PILLARS OF PENTEGARN
- #4   RETURN TO BROOKMERE
- #5   REVOLT OF THE DWARVES
- #6   REVENGE OF THE RAINBOW DRAGON
- #7   HERO OF WASHINGTON SQUARE
- #8   VILLAINS OF VOLTURNUS
- #9   ROBBERS AND ROBOTS
- #10   CIRCUS OF FEAR
- #11   SPELL OF THE WINTER WIZARD
- #12   LIGHT ON QUESTS MOUNTAIN
- #13   DRAGON OF DOOM
- #14   RAID ON NIGHTMARE CASTLE
- #15   UNDER DRAGON'S WING
- #16   THE DRAGON'S RANSOM
- #17   CAPTIVE PLANET
- #18   KING'S QUEST

For a free catalog, write
TSR, Inc.
P.O. Box 756, Dept. EQB
Lake Geneva, WI 53147